Mike Otis

"*Who* is *that*?" Paul whispered in awe.

"I don't know his name," Sheldon whispered back. "I think he's a senior. I've seen him around. Not the most outgoing guy in the world, I'd guess, but he looks like presidential timber to me."

"What? Are you crazy? You can't make that guy president!"

"Why not?"

"Well, first of all, because he'd never let you do it!"

Sheldon smiled wisely. "He won't have to know about it. We'll just file nomination papers on his behalf."

"But—But that can't happen—Can it?"

"I see no reason why not. We nominate him, wait a while, nobody else runs, and he's president. I don't think he'll mind. Of all the people in this school who don't care, I'd say he doesn't care the most."

Other books by GORDON KORMAN

DON'T CARE HIGH

Gordon Korman

SCHOLASTIC INC.

New York Toronto London Auckland Sydney

ISBN 0-590-40251-X

Copyright © 1985 by Gordon Korman.

12 11 10 9 8 7 6 5 4 3 2   6 7 8 9/8 0 1/9

For the real Mike Otis, wherever he may be.

And for Marilyn E. Marlow,
who helped me over the high fences.

"There are a lot of things at this school
I don't understand."

Mike Otis
Student Body President
Don Carey High School

1

Mr. Morrison beamed at his homeroom class of twenty-eight students. "Okay, are all the autobiographies finished?"

A vague, indifferent hum rose from the group.

"Good. When you bring your papers up to me, I can also check your class schedules to make sure there aren't any problems. I'm going to do the class in rows, starting from the left."

The entire class stood and began a lackadaisical shuffle toward the front of the room. Paul Abrams looked around in bewilderment. He was the only student still sitting. Hadn't the teacher said "starting from the left"? Maybe he'd heard the instructions wrong. He grabbed his schedule and his half-page autobiography and joined the swarm.

Mr. Morrison regarded the first person in line. "Well, where's your schedule?"

The girl dug through her pockets. "I didn't bring it. Maybe I didn't get one."

"But everybody got one. It was mailed to your house during the summer. You'll have to go to the office after homeroom and have a new one made up."

The girl looked dubious. "You think so?"

"Of course. How are you going to know what classes to go to if you don't have a schedule?"

"I figured I'd just sort of wing it."

Paul stared in disbelief. The second person in line didn't have a schedule either. The third had a schedule but it was somebody else's. The fourth was in the wrong homeroom. Paul was fifth, and the first to be checked through. He handed in his autobiography and returned to his seat, noting that Mr. Morrison was already covered in perspiration.

"What kind of schedule is this?" the teacher was exclaiming in agitation. "You're supposed to have six classes and a lunch! You have six lunches and a class!"

"Yeah?" The boy looked vaguely pleased. "That's pretty good."

"And you!" Mr. Morrison was already on to the next schedule. "You have no lunch at all! And you're going to the same Spanish class five times a day! You've had this for at least a month! Why didn't you check it over?"

"Maybe I didn't notice it."

Before Mr. Morrison could go on to the next student, she announced, "Mine's blank."

By the time the exercise was over, less than half the class had been checked through. The others were instructed to go to the office after homeroom and stand in the Problem Line. Paul couldn't believe the vacant, disinterested expressions on the faces of even those with serious class schedule conflicts, or no schedules at all.

Mr. Morrison had turned his attention to the autobiographies.

"Now we'll all get to know each other. I'm going to read them out loud. This first one here is by — " he glanced at the paper " — it looks like Wayne Stitsky. Stand up, Wayne."

In the very back row, a tall, slim boy with long blond, flyaway hair raised himself three inches from his chair and settled back down again. Mr. Morrison smiled and read:

" 'Hi. I'm Wayne-o. I'm in the tenth grade at Don't Care High — '" Mr. Morrison put the paper down. He looked up sternly. "Now, this is one thing I want to get straight right here on the first day of school. This is *not* Don't Care High. This is Don Carey High School. That awful nickname has been haunting this fine old school for years, and this is where it ends. We have pride and school spirit, and the maintaining of that self-destructive attitude of not caring is an insult to the memory of Don Carey, one of the most civic-minded public works commissioners this city has ever had. He was, as you all know, the designer and builder of our modern sewer system, and that is a remarkable contribution indeed."

Another hum rose just like the first.

"Now," Mr. Morrison went on, "we'll read a paper that doesn't have quite such a defeatist attitude." He began to shuffle through the stack, his brow clouding over, his mouth hardening into a thin line. "'Don't Care' 'Don't Care.' Ah, here we go. 'My name is Cindy Schwartz, and I'm fifteen years old, and it's been seven years since I started shopping at Bloomingdale's. I like Bloomingdale's because . . .'" He stopped reading and skipped his eyes down the page. "All right, where's Cindy? You didn't mention a word about school. This is all about Bloomingdale's."

There was an awkward silence, then someone called, "She left."

"Left? Why?"

"You told her to go to the office to get her schedule changed."

"But I said *after* — Oh, never mind." He returned to sifting through the autobiographies. "Here it is again. 'Don't Care High . . . Don't Care . . . Don't Care. . . . It looks like this group is going to take a lot of deprogramming. Ah, here's one. Paul Abrams. Where's Paul?"

Timidly, Paul raised his hand.

Mr. Morrison beamed anew. "Okay, let's see what you've got here. 'My name is Paul Abrams, and I originally come from Saskatoon, Saskatchewan. My family moved to New York over the summer, and I enrolled this morning at Don Carey High School.

4

I'm in the tenth grade, and it's my ambition to — '"

"Hey!" came a surprised voice from the back of the class. "Get a load of the guy with the ambition!"

The hum swelled again as Paul felt scarlet red creep up the back of his neck and flood his face.

Mr. Morrison rapped on his desk with a ruler. "Quiet down, everybody. I'd like to finish reading this paper. Then maybe you'll find out what a real Don Carey student should be like. This is exactly—"

Just then the public address system came alive with a voice that resembled the lower register of a bassoon.

May I have your attention, please. Welcome to another year of school. Just a few announcements. As you may or may not have noticed, this year's welcoming committee did not convene due to lack of interest.

A request from the cafeteria staff asks me to remind you that there are garbage cans strategically placed in the dining area.

It has been brought to my attention that, while some students must do without, some of you have as many as eight or nine lockers. This seems excessive.

Also, we'll be accepting nominations for student body president as of today. Normally this process would have taken place last spring, but again, due to lack of interest, no names were entered, rendering the election redundant. In a fit of optimism, we have decided to try again.

Finally, due to the disrepair of clocks in this school, I would ask that everyone synchronize watches. It is now fifteen seconds to first period. That's all. Have a good day.

Paul watched as the class stood up and began to file out the door. He looked for a signal from Mr. Morrison that class was dismissed, but the teacher had returned to some paperwork. Tentatively, he rose.

"Hey, Ambition, aren't you coming?"

Paul's attention shifted to the doorway where a husky, sandy-haired boy stood watching him. Paul scowled. Only an hour into the school year, and already he was the butt of jokes.

The boy laughed. "Don't look at me like that. I'm harmless. It's just that anyone with ambition is going to need a guide around this place. At this time of the year, everyone's ambition is Christmas vacation. After that, they wait till June."

Still wary, Paul picked up his notebook and followed the other boy into the hallway.

"The name's Sheldon Pryor." He looked at Paul intently. "You do talk, don't you?"

Paul grinned. "Yeah, I talk. I'm almost afraid to, though, in this place. What's wrong with ambition?"

Sheldon laughed. "Seeing as how you're new here, I'll lay the cards right on the table. Morrison's wrong. This is not Don Carey High School. This is Don't Care High. It's more than a nickname — it's a

6

concept. The school spirit here is so low that it's off the scale. There are twenty-six hundred kids roaming around these halls, and I defy you to find me one of them who gives a hoot about anything school-related." Paul looked dubious. "And it's all contagious. The school doesn't care about the community, so the community doesn't care about the school, so the board lets the place get all run down because they know that nobody cares."

"No offense," said Paul, "but I don't think I can believe that."

Sheldon laughed. "You want proof? Look at that teacher over there." He indicated a thin, cadaverous man standing in front of a classroom, a distant expression in his eyes. "That's Mr. Knight. Five years ago he was teaching in the suburbs. They called him 'Super Teacher.' He was known everywhere as the guy who could motivate a rock." Sheldon shook his head sadly. "But then, you know, you're riding on top of the world, and you get cocky. Maybe he said the wrong thing to a school board member, or took someone's parking place, but whatever the reason, they transferred him to Don't Care High. Now he's a zombie like everybody else. They say the only thing he cares about is his European bottle cap collection."

Paul frowned. "How could he have changed like that? He might have found different kinds of kids here, but he should still stay the same kind of teacher."

"Simple," Sheldon replied. "His whole style was class discussion. He had to take all sides of every argument because no one else participated, and from this he developed a multiple personality. After a few years, he took some time off for psychiatric examination, and when he came back, he was like this. He picked up the bottle cap thing from a fellow patient."

"Mr. Morrison isn't a zombie," Paul pointed out. "He seems to care."

"You can't go by Morrison. He's the guidance counselor, which makes him the loneliest guy in the building. He's so desperate for someone to talk to that he sees some fancy high-priced analyst uptown who motivates him to motivate us."

Paul laughed. "I thought guidance would be really busy in a big school like this."

"Nope. No one wants counseling. Don't Care has no problems — none worth caring about, anyway. We never even had anybody with ambition until today. Besides, the guidance office is three-quarters filled up with old, unused application forms." Sheldon glanced at his watch. "We'd better start walking if we're going to be ten minutes late. You've got English next, right?"

"Yeah. How'd you know?"

"Most of the people from our homeroom are in that class. You see, we don't have course selection here anymore."

"But every school has course selection," Paul protested.

"Yeah, well, not this one. Nobody fills out the cards. And they can't force people to pick, so they just assign classes. They did it to you, didn't they?"

"Well, yes, but I figured because I was registering late — "

"Oh no. It's policy. The word is a couple of years ago they asked some girl if she wanted to take industrial arts, cooking, or infrared astronomy, and she said, 'What's the difference?' They dumped selection for the whole school right on the spot."

As they navigated the hallways, Paul's eyes examined the passing parade. His new fellow students were making their lethargic ways in various directions, drifting in and out of classrooms, to and from lockers, and scanning bulletin boards with great disinterest. There wasn't a school jacket or school letter in sight. And, Paul thought, glancing at his notebook, he was apparently the only one who had bothered to bring something to write on. The people themselves were physically no different from the students at Kilgour Secondary School back home in Saskatoon — except for the eyes. The Don Carey students seemed to have their eyes focused on infinity, or at least on some place outside the walls of the school. Their behavior was normal enough. They talked, moved, laughed. But if eyes were the windows of the soul, these people had their blinds drawn. All except Sheldon.

"How about you?" Paul asked, following his new guide through the shabby cream-colored halls. "You seem to care."

"Oh, I only came in halfway through last year," Sheldon replied airily, "so I still care a little. I don't know how long it'll last, though. This morning I went into the washroom to visit Don Carey's big invention — I figure as a student here it's my duty to patronize the sewer system every now and then — and someone had written 'Who Cares?' on the wall. Underneath it — I counted them — forty people wrote 'Not me'. So I was looking at it, and for one brief moment it seemed so right. Then the room went out of focus, and when I came back to myself, there were forty-one 'Not me's' on that wall." He smiled engagingly. "It'll happen to you too, Ambition."

Paul laughed nervously. "The name's Paul. And I don't freak out that easily."

"We'll see. Right turn."

They entered English class right on time ten minutes late, and were among the first to arrive. The subject was Shakespeare's *Hamlet*, and while Paul tried to concentrate, he found himself marveling at how the teacher seemed unperturbed by the fact that her students were trickling in twenty, thirty, even forty minutes late, and in the case of Wayne-o from homeroom, a scant seven minutes before the end of the hour.

". . .and these are some of the things I'd like you to keep in mind when you read the play," the teacher was saying as Paul watched Wayne-o establish himself at a last row desk. "Any questions?"

Paul, who wanted to ask if the school library had multiple copies of *Hamlet*, raised his hand. A surprised hum swelled in the classroom.

"Bad move, Ambition," came a whisper from Sheldon.

Paul felt the red returning to his face. Meanwhile, the teacher, who had turned away secure in the knowledge that there would be no questions, looked back to discover the source of the murmur.

"Yes? You have a question?"

"Oh . . . uh . . . no. Not me. No question."

"Your hand's still up," whispered Sheldon.

Painfully aware that he was once more the center of attention, Paul nonchalantly swung his raised hand over to scratch his forehead. The hum faded.

The morning progressed, and deep shock set in as the former student of Kilgour Secondary, Saskatoon, made his way through Don't Care High, Manhattan. He walked through the alien halls feeling like a visitor from Mars, watching the natives drift about aimlessly, and marveling at some of the sheets tacked up on bulletin boards:

SIGN UP HERE TO HELP KNIT AFGHANS FOR
BLITZ-TORN ENGLAND

It was dated 1941, and in its forty-four years of posting, had not managed to attract a single volunteer.

Underneath that:

MAYOR LAGUARDIA NEEDS YOUR HELP!
STUDENTS FOR A CLEANER NEW YORK

Paul sighed. Not only did no one care enough to sign up for these things, but no one could even be bothered to take the notices down when they became obsolete. What a place.

As he entered his geography class, he heard a voice call out, "Hey, Ambition. Over here." There at a back row desk was Sheldon Pryor, smiling and waving. Paul joined him, grateful to see a familiar face.

Mrs. Wolfe began the class with what she called a geography game. "Now, I want everybody to participate." The hum swelled. "You've each got a card with the name of a country and several clues describing that country's industries. When I call on you, you read out the clues, but not the name of the country. That's for the class to guess. For example, if I were to say that a country was the biggest producer of steel in the world, you would of course say the United States. You see?" Dead silence. "Okay, let's start with — " she consulted her class list — "Dan Wilburforce."

Dan concentrated on his card. "Uruguay."

"No, no, no! I *told* you to read only the clues! We're supposed to *guess* what country it is!"

"Oh. Okay. Woolen, cotton, and rayon textile manufacturing, meat processing, cement manufacturing — "

Mrs. Wolfe was getting desperate. "What's the point? We already know — "

A hand shot up. "Venezuela?" came a wild guess.

"All right, all right!" exclaimed Mrs. Wolfe. "Forget the game. We'll just read the cards as a point of interest. Who's got Brazil?" There was no anwer. "Well, come on! Somebody's got Brazil. I handed it out." Still nothing. "Look, people, this is impossible! Someone has Brazil!"

Mrs. Wolfe became so upset that she began to march up and down between the rows of desks, checking each card. She stopped before one boy and completely blew her stack.

"You! You've got Brazil! Why didn't you say something?"

The boy looked confused. "But you said we shouldn't tell."

The door burst open and Wayne-o breezed in. "Hi. Did I miss anything?"

"We played a game," Dan Wilburforce announced blandly.

Mrs. Wolfe screamed, but no one seemed to notice.

Sheldon leaned over to Paul. "Come on, Ambition, don't look so freaked out. Think how funny this is."

"Mom, I'm home." Paul staggered in the door of apartment 3305, his ears still popping from the high-speed elevator.

"I'm in the kitchen, dear."

Paul tossed his coat unceremoniously over a chair and headed through the apartment, mentally planning out his sob story for maximum effect. He decided to start with:

"Mom, I've got to talk to you about this school you've sent me to!" As he entered the kitchen, he saw his mother taking a cake out of the oven.

"Well, how was it? I'm dying to hear about your first day."

"Well, Mom, it's like this . . . ." He paused. Should he talk about the dilapidated building that was fated to come down upon his head sometime between now and graduation, or should he concentrate on the zombies who hummed every time anything school-related was mentioned? And what about the "Don't Care" thing? She probably wouldn't believe it anyway. He only half believed it

13

himself. "This school isn't like Kilgour, Mom. It's kind of — "

A high-pitched beeping cut the air. Paul winced as his mother went to answer the phone. He wondered what was so wrong with the old kind that just rang. It had probably taken a team of scientists five years and several million dollars to develop a sound so irritating to the nerves.

"Hello? . . . Oh, hello, Nancy . . . No, I'm not busy at all. I've just finished some baking."

Paul groaned inwardly. Auntie Nancy. Now there was a sore point and a half. It had been Auntie Nancy who had convinced his father to apply for a job in New York. Auntie Nancy had organized the whole move. Auntie Nancy, who was snug in a ranch house on Long Island, had arranged for this apartment up in the clouds; Auntie Nancy was responsible for placing the family in the attendance district for Don't Care High.

"So, Nancy, did Harry let you order the dishwasher? . . . No? But did you explain to him that you're the only house on the block with no dishwasher? . . . Oh, he's so stubborn, that husband of yours."

Paul wandered out of the kitchen, feeling a slight shred of satisfaction that his Auntie Nancy was not getting the dishwasher she had been nagging for as long as he could remember. He straggled into his room and went to stand listlessly by the window. Thirty-three floors below, the rush hour traffic jam was assuming its usual mammoth proportions. A Volkswagen had rear-ended a limousine, and the two drivers seemed to be squaring off, cheered on by a bus stop full of people. Coupled with the construction on the road, the accident made the street impassable. The honking of horns and the barrage of jackhammers wafted up to his aerie. He slammed the window shut and gazed through the glass at the apartment building across the street. That was always a lively showcase. A few floors below, a woman was shaking her mop out the window in proud defiance of all city ordinances. Directly above her, a man in goggles was welding something to a large metal contraption that looked like a chrome torpedo. The man paused in his work, seemed to see Paul, and immediately closed the blinds.

Through the wall he could hear his mother still on the telephone. It seemed to be shaping up into one of their longer conversations. He decided to postpone his case against Don't Care High for at least a few days. He could already hear the "You haven't even given it a chance yet" lecture, one of his mother's favorites. Then his father would deliver the crowning touch with "Life is what you make it." It was a devastating combination.

He threw himself backwards onto his bed to mull over his first day at Don't Care High. Of his classes, Sheldon was in two, and he was beginning to recognize some of the familiar faces from homeroom in the others. The most prominent of these was Wayne-o, who was apparently registered for all six, yet on time for none. The best prospect for a friend was definitely Sheldon, who was certainly amicable enough, and the only student Paul had yet encountered who cared about anything. Sheldon had even promised to arrange things with Feldstein, the major locker baron of the school, so that Paul could have a locker instead of living out of a plastic bag.

He sighed. It looked like, for the next little while, he would just have to see what happened.

2

Feldstein looked like a normal person, Paul thought. He must have been an exception to the rule at Don't Care High, since he seemed to care about at least one thing — lockers. The locker baron hung out in the first floor east stairwell at all times when he wasn't in class. There he sat in majesty in an old armchair with the stuffing bleeding out of it, nestled beneath a flight of stairs.

"You know Paul from our homeroom," said Sheldon.

Feldstein looked blank. "Who?"

"The guy with ambition."

"Oh, yeah — cool. How many lockers do you need, man?"

"Uh . . . one is just fine," said Paul.

Feldstein looked a little shocked. "Just one? Okay." From his pocket he produced a map of the school hallways with his many holdings indicated in red. "It's a tight deal this year, and I couldn't get a lot of the good locations. But I have got one with a southern exposure. At about quarter of two, the sun is reflecting off the windows across the street right at this little baby. Interested?"

"We'll take it," said Sheldon decisively. "It's just down the hall from mine."

"Zero—forty-two—two," said Feldstein, quoting the combination from memory. "It's number 746B. Enjoy."

"Thanks . . . uh . . . Feldstein," said Paul. "I guess I'll be seeing you in homeroom."

Feldstein shook his head. "No, man."

"Feldstein's not too big on homeroom," Sheldon supplied. "He has a lot of business responsibilities."

"Oh, well, what do I owe you for the locker?"

"Forget it, man. You'll pay me later."

"Oh no. I have money."

"Not money," said Feldstein in disgust. "I just did you a favor; someday maybe you can do me a favor."

Paul opened his mouth to protest, but Sheldon burst in with, "Thanks a lot, Feldstein. See you around."

As they made their way toward homeroom, Paul complained nervously to his companion. "Why did you get me into this? I don't want to owe that guy a favor! He's some kind of gangster!"

Sheldon just laughed. "He's harmless as a puppy. He called in my favor last year. You know what it was? He needed a cake. You know why? Because he was hungry. Big gangster."

May I have your attention, please. The sun is shining, and therefore the ventilation system has malfunctioned. It is now eighty degrees at the airport, and ninety degrees in the school halls, with a relative humidity of ninety-eight percent, and prevailing winds coming from the music room. If any of you feel any dizzier than usual, I would like to remind you that we have a medical office on the basement level.

You may or may not be pleased to know that the Varsity Basketball League has decided to allow us teams this year on the condition that we accept no home games due to lackluster attendance in previous seasons. Tryouts for the boys' varsity begin this afternoon at three-thirty. I'd better add that the team needs at least five players to have a reasonable chance of winning any games.

First period commences in three minutes. That's all. Have a good day.

"Who *is* that guy?" Paul whispered to Sheldon.

"Oh, him? That's the principal," Sheldon replied. "Mr. . . . uh . . . Mr. . . . " he slapped his forehead. "I used to know it. Mr. — "

"Doesn't he sign all the official notices home?" Paul caught the look on Sheldon's face. "You're not trying to tell me there aren't any notices here."

"We had a notice once last year, but I think it came from Morrison. I don't think anybody brought one home, though. As I recall, the janitorial staff used it as grounds for a pay hike."

Mr. Morrison stood up behind his desk. "Okay, it's time for class. Don't forget the guidance office is open to all of you until four o'clock every day."

A dull hum greeted this announcement, and the class began to disperse.

The only noteworthy event of the morning for Paul came in second period — chemistry class — when he was introduced to his lab partner for the year, Daphne Sylvester. At six-foot-one, blonde, and stunning, she seemed designed to make him feel as insignificant as a dust mote in a typhoon. He slaved over the day's experiment while she sat passively by, signifying her approval, he figured, by not falling asleep. The only thing which seemed to catch her interest briefly was when Wayne-o, making his customary late entrance, struck the teacher, Mr. Schmidt, with the door, sending him sprawling into a shelf of glass beakers. This event caused quite a hum in the lab. Mr. Schmidt decided to mark Wayne-o absent.

"Oh, you got Daphne, huh?" Sheldon commented as he and Paul wandered through the halls after lunch. "Quite a pick."

"It was the luck of the draw," said Paul glumly. "Talk about your silent partner. The girl is dead. I don't know whether to do an experiment or an autopsy. I tried to check her eyes for signs of life, but the angle was too great. I'm getting a kink in my neck."

"What can I say? She's typical. She isn't dead; she just doesn't care. You're going to have to adjust to the fact that the different one isn't Daphne. It's you."

"I'm starting to get the picture," Paul sighed, sitting down on a window ledge. "You know, at my old school, they told us we were the citizens of tomorrow."

"They'd never do that here," said Sheldon. "It'd be too depressing. But as near as I can tell, people do learn things here. I don't know how it happens, but it happens. There are bad grades and there are good grades, but Don't Care students graduate."

"But why is it like this? The 'Don't Care' thing, I mean?"

Sheldon shrugged. "It's hard to say. It could be Manhattan, but there are perfectly normal schools not a mile away. It could be this one hundred forty-year-old building, but there are worse, I guess. Maybe it's the legacy of Don Carey and his sewage. But look. Look behind you out the window. What do you see?"

Paul swiveled and squinted through the unwashed glass. "Looks like a highway interchange."

"Right," said Sheldon. "It's the 22nd Street ramp for the Henry Hudson Parkway. It also happens to be Don't Care High's athletic field. Look, you can still see one of the goalposts in the center of the cloverleaf. They had to cut off the left upright to make room for the right lane merge. And if you look real hard, you can see the fifty-yard line by the base of that parking garage."

"But how did that happen?"

"Well, the story goes that twelve years ago, when the city wanted somewhere around here to put their new ramp, it just so happened that the school board was looking for real estate to build a fancy new school uptown. So they gambled that, at Don't Care High, no one would notice, let alone care. Don't Care always concentrated on basketball rather than football anyway, since it's a lot easier to find five players than twelve. So they traded our playing field for the uptown land. Anyway, a few years later they started a subway tunnel under there, but ran out of money, and eventually the ground caved in. So they paved it, all but that little patch around the fifty-yard line."

Paul's face flamed red. "That's ridiculous! What kind of city would do that?"

"Oh, the city would have backed down if there had been any kind of protest. But this is Don't Care High — "

"It's terrible, that's what it is!" Paul interrupted hotly. "All this school needs is someone to take care of its interests, someone to represent it!"

Sheldon looked mildly amused. "Why not you? Want to be student body president?"

"Are you crazy? It's my second day in the school. No one knows me."

"That's no problem. It's not as though there's going to be an election or anything like that. We just nominate you, and you win unopposed."

"And then what?"

"Oh, nothing, of course," said Sheldon. "No one can do anything with this place."

"Forget it," said Paul. "I don't want to be president just because nobody cares enough to run against me. Why don't *you* run?"

"No way," said Sheldon quickly, "I'm strictly a behind-the-scenes man. But I think you're right. It *is* about time someone took over the reins of power around here." His eyes scanned the near-deserted hallway and lit on a lone figure standing in front of a locker. "Him, for instance."

Paul stared in shock. There at the end of Sheldon's gaze stood a bizarre character, motionless by his open locker. He was of medium height, slight, and very dark, with an olive complexion. His straight black hair was slicked back from his forehead, giving him a weasel-like appearance, which was accentuated further by his beady black eyes. His posture was terrible, combining a slump with a forward tilt, and he wore a voluminous, full-length, dull-beige raincoat which hung on him as if on a bent coat hanger. Beneath his open coat he wore a pink shirt and jeans which were turned up tightly at the ankles. Each cuff was secured with a large safety pin. On his feet were glossy black dress shoes.

"*Who* is *that*?" Paul whispered in awe.

"I don't know his name," Sheldon whispered back. "I think he's a senior. I've seen him around. Not the most outgoing guy in the world, I'd guess, but he looks like presidential timber to me."

"What? Are you crazy? You can't make that guy president!"

"Why not?"

"Well, first of all, because he'd never let you do it!"

Sheldon smiled wisely. "He won't have to know about it. We'll just file nomination papers on his behalf."

"But — But that can't happen — Can it?"

"I see no reason why not. We nominate him, wait a while, nobody else runs, and he's president. I don't think he'll mind. Of all the people in this school who don't care, I'd say he doesn't care the most. I mean, it isn't as though he'd have to do anything."

Paul shook his head. "But don't you think he'll complain when he finds out he's president?"

"He might, but I doubt it. From what I can tell about him, he'll probably just ignore the whole thing. We've got a problem, though. We don't know his name. We can't just nominate him as the guy with greased-back hair and safety pins in his pants."

Paul looked back at the apparition, who was still standing and staring into his locker. Him? President? "Well, I guess that's it then. You don't know his name, so you can't do it. Too bad."

"Follow me," said Sheldon. With Paul tagging along cautiously, he approached the boy in the raincoat. "Hi. I've seen you around here a lot. I'm Shel, and this is Paul."

The black eyes remained blank. The response was quiet and dry. "Hi."

Sheldon waited for more and, when none came, added, "I don't think we know your name."

The boy looked at him again. "I don't think so either," he said in an unpunctuated monotone. He shut his locker door and snapped on the lock. "Bye." Then he was gone, hunching down the hallway, headed for the stairwell.

"What *was* that?" asked Paul in awe.

Sheldon was impressed, too. "He's something special, even for this school. But you've got to admit that he's perfect to represent the students of Don't Care High."

Paul laughed. "All right, Sheldon, let's drop it. You can't make that guy president. You can't even get him to identify himself."

"I'll find out who he is. Somebody must know him."

Rosalie Gladstone shrugged almost expansively enough to dislocate both shoulders, then snapped her gum three times. "What do you want to know that for?" Her voice seemed to operate on the same frequency as Paul's mother's telephone.

Sheldon put on his most charming smile and treated the question as rhetorical. "But you *have* seen him?"

"Oh, sure. I guess. I don't know." She laughed.

Peter Eversleigh was not much help, either. He sat cross-legged in front of his locker, taking precise, rhythmic, quarter-inch bites out of a long string of black licorice. He looked up at Sheldon and Paul.

"Yeah, I know the dude about whom you are

speaking. Greased-back hair, raincoat, jeans with safety pins. Must be one conceptual dude."

"Oh, he is," said Sheldon. "Do you happen to know his name?"

"Neg, dude. No name."

Even Wayne-o had no idea, commenting, "Well, he's a senior, and he's weird, and he drives a cool car. But I don't know his name. It's not Wayne-o, though. That's me." He walked away, laughing as though he'd just said something hilarious.

"Well, I guess your man's political career is on the skids already," said Paul, mostly out of relief. "He's the most anonymous person I've ever heard of. Why don't you try making Wayne-o president? Everybody knows him."

"Wayne-o would never want to be president," Sheldon explained patiently. "He's just happy that he gets to be Wayne-o. But we're not dead yet. We've got one more chance." He headed for the stairwell.

Paul followed reluctantly. "Aw no, Shel, not Feldstein! I want to steer clear of that guy. If he gives us information, he's going to want another favor."

"This one's on me," Sheldon promised with a grin.

As they descended into the locker baron's lair, they found Feldstein already occupied with a redhaired boy, one in the junior class.

"Last January you needed a locker by the art room — I got you a locker by the art room. Today I need a favor from you."

"What'll it be, Feldstein?"

"Mashed potatoes, I need mashed potatoes — smooth, creamy, not instant. With chicken gravy."

"You've got it, Feldstein." The junior ran off.

Sheldon stepped forward.

Feldstein looked surprised. "You're back already? Is something wrong with the locker?"

"Oh no," Paul stammered. "It's fine."

"We need information," said Sheldon. "A name. His locker's 205C."

Feldstein shook his head, his face assuming a world-weary expression. "No, man, not that guy. I lost a lot of sleep over that guy."

Paul had to speak up. "Why?"

A distant gleam flickered in the locker baron's eye. "Last year I went for broke. I owned the entire 200C series, the longest uninterrupted row of lockers in the school — except for 205. So I made a play for 205. That's how I first met Mike Otis."

"Mike Otis?" repeated Paul.

"Mike Otis!" cheered Sheldon, waving a fist in triumph. "He's going to be a great man!"

Feldstein looked pained. "I sent for the guy — he didn't come! *I* had to find *him*! It took me *three days* hanging out in front of 205. *Twice* the janitors tried to throw out my chair while I was away. So finally I found him." He looked Sheldon squarely in the eye. "Have you ever actually tried to *talk* to Mike Otis? Forget it! I would have had more chance making a deal with his locker. I offered him locker packages fit for royalty. He wasn't interested. My best locations! With views! Convenient to almost any room he wanted! No. And that was it — the end of the biggest locker bid in history. I could have retired on those 200C's. I'm not getting any younger, you know. So don't talk to me about Mike Otis."

Sheldon placed a sympathetic hand on the locker baron's shoulder. "You're still the greatest of them all, Feldstein. Thanks for the name. I owe you."

At three thirty-five that afternoon, the name of Mike Otis was officially placed in the running for the position of student body president of Don Carey High School. There were twenty-five names in support of the nomination. These had been easily collected from students Sheldon was friendly with. While no one was interested in signing, no one was willing to put up any resistance, either, and Sheldon pressed this advantage.

"Here, sign this," he would say.

"Why?"

"Why not?" This was the turning point.

The submission was placed in the box at the guidance office, so the first person to see it the next morning was Mr. Morrison. Excitedly, he dashed off to the main office to spread the good news that the school, leaderless for so long, would once again have a student body president. He rushed in the door, waving the sheet at Mr. Gamble, the vice-principal.

Mr. Gamble was unimpressed. "Well, obviously it's a hoax. I know that Otis boy."

"Well yes," Mr. Morrison admitted. "Mike is a little reserved. That's why his running for president is such a golden opportunity in terms of his development."

Mrs. Carling, one of the school secretaries, came over to examine the nomination paper. "Son-of-a-gun. I've been here nine years, and I've never seen one of these before."

"It's a joke," Mr. Gamble insisted. "There's no way that Otis boy would take the time and effort to run."

"At this school," called another secretary, "there's no way anyone would take the time and effort to play a joke."

This caused a hush.

"Well, all the signers are registered students," said Mr. Morrison defensively. "I'm treating this as a legitimate nomination."

Gamble sighed. "I suppose we have to. But mark my words, we're going to look pretty stupid over this."

May I have your attention, please. Here are the day's announcements.

Our volleyball team, the Don Carey Sewer Men, is in desperate need of a new name, as they've found that the old one is not conducive to finishing anywhere but in the toilet. Also, we seem to have misplaced the net. Anyone with any ideas or equipment to contribute should see Coach Murphy. And may I remind you that the team still needs four players.

As may have become apparent, last year's yearbook project was shelved due to lack of interest. We are hoping to do a double book this year, and are seeking

*volunteers early. Anyone interested, see
Mr. Morrison.*

*Finally, I am pleased to announce that
the name of Mike Otis has been entered
in nomination for student body president.*

A great hum of shock swelled in the homerooms
and filled the halls. In Mr. Morrison's class, Paul
tried to look as surprised as everyone else, while
sensing deep in his heart that disaster would be the
only result of this roller coaster that Sheldon had
started them on. Sheldon himself was beaming
with pride, and Mr. Morrison marched up and
down between the rows of desks, looking into faces
and saying,

"Did you hear that? Did you hear that?"

Mike Otis happened to be late for school that
morning, thereby missing the announcement
altogether.

*Nominations close at the end of this
week, and I would like to point out that,
if we get one more name, we will be able
to have an all-candidates meeting.*

That's all. Have a good day.

Paul ushered Sheldon in the door of apartment
3305. "Hey, Mom, I'm home. I've brought a friend."

They found Mrs. Abrams bustling about the
kitchen, her purse over her shoulder, the car keys
in her hand.

"Mom, this is Sheldon Pryor from Don't — from school."

Paul's mother smiled distractedly. "Very nice to meet you, Sheldon. Paul, I'm glad you're home. I've got some instructions for you. I have to go out right away. Your Auntie Nancy had a terrible experience today. She was having her hair streaked, and the timer malfunctioned. It all turned green!"

"Is she okay?"

"Yes, but she's terribly upset. She spent all day at the beauty parlor, but the green is still there. She asked me to come over and sit with her. Now, I won't be home until late, and your father has meetings tonight, but there's a roast in the oven. Turn it off at four-thirty, eat what you want, and wrap the rest up. Sherman is welcome to join you if it's okay with his mother."

"That's Sheldon, Mom."

"Yes, of course. Good-bye, boys. Be careful you don't burn your fingers on the roasting pan." She bustled out.

"Your Mom seems a little uptight," Sheldon commented.

"Yeah, well, she's okay. She just has to adjust to the new place and all that."

Sheldon surveyed his surroundings. "Nice apartment. Pretty high up. How's the view?"

"Concrete," said Paul. "Now, why don't we have a Coke, go into the living room, put on some music, and talk about why you went nuts and nominated Mike Otis for president?"

"It's not such a big thing," said Sheldon. "On

Monday they'll declare him president, and it's business as usual. Nothing changes at Don't Care High. Thanks." He accepted a tall frosted glass.

The two retired to the living room and established themselves comfortably on the rug. Paul switched on the radio and turned to his friend. "So it's over, right? The Mike Otis thing, I mean?"

"Sure. Okay, it caused a stir in homeroom, but you'll notice nobody mentioned it after that. There'll be some more humming when they declare him president, that's all. Anyway, when are you going to start your map for geography — the one due next week?"

"Oh, I did mine last night."

Sheldon's brow clouded. "If we're going to be friends, Ambition, you're going to have to pick up a few poor work habits." He looked thoughtful. "Or I might have to pick up some good ones. What a revolting thought."

Paul laughed. They joked about school, tore into a bag of potato chips, and toasted Mike Otis with Coke until the radio announcer's voice brought them back to earth:

"You're listening to Flash Flood on Stereo 99, creeping up on the dinner hour. We've got some new Stones coming up, but first a traffic report. Stay home. It's a mess out there. It's five-thirty in the greatest city in the world, and — "

"The roast!" cried Paul, jumping up and running for the kitchen. There was a short pause, then, "Sheldon?"

"Yeah?"

"The roast's on fire, Sheldon!"

Sheldon ran into the kitchen, shouting instructions. "Don't throw water on it! It's a grease fire! Smother it! Keep close to the floor! Wet a towel — "

"It's out," interrupted Paul, donning padded mitts and removing the roasting pan from the smoky oven. "It went out by itself. But look at the roast!"

Both boys stared at the charred lump which had once been dinner.

"A little well-done," Sheldon observed. He beamed. "But I know a place not far from here where they make a bowl of chili that bites back. Interested?"

"What about the roast?" mourned Paul.

Sheldon shrugged. "Ashes to ashes. Come on. Let's go."

Paul lay in bed, reexperiencing his dinner over and over again. What went by the name of New York chili would have been labeled DANGER: HIGHLY CORROSIVE back home. Not only did this chili bite back, but it would probably still be undigested at the autopsy.

His agony aside, the evening had been quite unremarkable. He'd had a good time with Sheldon, his father had come home and dropped off to sleep on the sofa, and Auntie Nancy had calmed down after a fashion, pending a promise from her hairdresser that she would be blonde again tomorrow. Even the lecture for burning the roast had been relatively short.

Finding sleep impossible, he went to the window to check on the building across the street. One thirty in the morning, and at least half the lights were on. Somewhere around the twenty-eighth or twenty-ninth floor, five fat bald men with cigars, looking like identical quintuplets, sat around a small table, playing cards. Paul gawked at the mountains of money sitting in front of them. Even in the unlikely event that all of those bills were ones, there would still be enough cash there to buy and sell Paul Abrams several times over.

One floor up and to the right, a group of young people were assembling a Volkswagen in a completely furnished living room. Beside them, a woman was washing her windows. At this hour? Paul watched in amazement as she finished the inside, climbed out onto the four-inch ledge, and nonchalantly began washing the outside, apparently unworried about the several-hundred-foot drop to the street.

It was too much. He crawled back into bed, but found himself concentrating on the late movie, which was playing on the TV set next door. Whoever lived there was apparently a night owl, and obviously quite deaf.

Paul sighed.

3

Classes were classes to Paul, and differed very little from those he had taken at Kilgour, his last high school. A class at Don't Care was quieter (except for the occasional hum) and had far less student participation, but the material itself seemed constant. It ranged from uninteresting to mildly interesting — or at least, as Sheldon put it, "interesting, in a boring sort of way."

Paul's last class of the day was photography. It was his most interesting course, not because of the subject matter, but rather because of the motley group it attracted. It was the only one of Paul's courses which was not restricted to tenth graders, and provided him with the opportunity to view the Don't Care student at all stages of his development in his unnatural habitat: the classroom.

It was the final hour of the week, the lecture was on the correct mixing of developing chemicals, and Paul's mind had wandered to Mike Otis when the candidate himself appeared at the back of the class. It was a jolt for Paul to see him there, partly a jab of conscience and partly the fact that the elusive Mike was normally so difficult to pin down.

Mr. Willis interrupted his lecture to look inquiringly at the apparition in the voluminous raincoat. "May I help you?"

"I don't think so," replied Mike, slithering into the seat directly behind Paul.

Mr. Willis dried his hands on a towel. "Well — are you registered for this class?"

"Yes."

"Would you mind telling me where you've been all week?"

The monotone was perfect. "It's taken me a few days to get my act together."

Mr. Willis consulted his class list. "Could I trouble you to tell me your name?"

"Mike Otis."

Paul braced himself for the hum, but none came. Apparently, the announcement of the candidacy had been forgotten.

Mr. Willis continued his demonstration, but now in a state of obvious distraction. As he mixed the various powders and liquids, his eyes kept darting toward the back of the classroom where his newest pupil sat. This went on for five minutes, until he slammed down a bottle of Photo-Flo in obvious agitation and cried,

"Good God, man, it's like a sauna in here! Why don't you take off that raincoat?"

"I'd rather not," said Mike.

The teacher was just returning painfully to the lesson when Wayne-o burst in the door. "Am I late?"

"Only forty minutes," Mr. Willis breathed, beginning to gather up his chemicals. "It's very warm in here. Class dismissed. Next week we'll start shooting."

"Shooting?" came a worried voice in the general shuffle that followed.

"Shooting *pictures*!" howled Mr. Willis in exasperation. "This is photography!"

And as Paul left the room, he knew with a feeling of great sympathy that this semester was not going to be an easy one for poor Mr. Willis.

Sheldon lived in Greenwich Village in an elegant old townhouse about ten blocks southwest of Paul's apartment building. He was on the corner to meet Paul that Saturday afternoon.

"It's different here than where you live," Sheldon was saying as they walked. "You can see the sky." He indicated a sickly little tree that was sticking up through a hole in the sidewalk. "Look. Greenbelt."

Paul grinned. "You're sure it's okay with your folks that I come over today?"

"Oh, sure. Nobody's home except my sister Jodi. And she'll be in the bathroom anyway, just in case I have to use it."

They walked up half a dozen stone steps to a

small wooden door. Sheldon unlocked it and ushered Paul inside.

"We're here!" he called out. "This will be your last warning!" To Paul, he said, "My dad's at the ball game with my kid brother, and my mom's working today."

"I'm in the bathroom," called a girl's voice from upstairs.

"Your mom works Saturdays?"

"Yeah, well, she's a genius. Or at least that's what everybody says she is, which means she has to work weekends."

"My parents are visiting my aunt and uncle today," said Paul. "That's my Auntie Nancy. You remember her — the one with the green hair."

They went into the living room and Sheldon switched on the radio. "Do you realize," he said, "that at this very moment, Mike Otis is our leader? Nominations closed yesterday, remember?"

Paul made a face. "Yeah, I know. And don't forget you promised that, as soon as they declare him president on Monday, that's the end of it."

Sheldon shrugged. "We fulfilled our roles as kingmakers. What else is there?"

"Nothing, I guess."

They sat for a few minutes listening to Flash Flood rant and rave about a new album. Jodi came in to stir up some interest in milk shakes, and the three adjourned to the kitchen.

Paul watched his friend's sister as she scooped ice cream into the blender, chattering engagingly about her own school and her impressions of the eighth grade. This wonderful, happy, energetic, aware person, he reflected, was less than a year away from the bizarre, indifferent halls of Don't Care High.

When Mr. Morrison advised the class to pay special attention to the announcements on Monday morning, Paul knew that it had happened. He had known it would happen anyway, but there was always that chance, however slight, that there would be another candidate. Not now. He caught a sideways grin of triumph from Sheldon as the principal came over the P.A.:

> *May I have your attention, please. There is only one announcement this morning. Mike Otis is now the president of your student body.*

The now-familiar hum swelled throughout the school.

> *The transition of power was very smooth in spite of the fact that there has not been a president since 1956. Mr. Gamble is anxious to meet with Mike Otis at his convenience. Congratulations, Mike. That's all. Have a good day.*

"Excellent!" Sheldon was declaring as homeroom broke up and the students began to disperse for first period. "Didn't it sound great when Mr. What's-his-name announced him president? Oh wow!"

"Shut up, Shel! Someone'll hear you!" muttered Paul through clenched teeth.

"So what? The whole world should know! We have a president! A sovereign! A charismatic hero!"

"He has about as much charisma as a picket fence!" Paul pointed out. "And the only things heroic about him are the safety pins in his pants."

Sheldon was undaunted. "Hey, Wayne-o, what do you think about Mike Otis being president?"

Wayne-o looked blank. "Who?"

"Mike Otis!"

"What about him?"

"He's student body president!"

"Oh." Wayne-o drifted off.

Paul was relieved. "You were right, Shel. Absolutely nobody cares."

"But they've got to care!" Sheldon blurted out.

"Now wait a minute! You were the guy who said that this was all over when they announced he was president. Well, that just happened, so it's finished. Right?"

"Technically, yes," Sheldon admitted.

"Now just what does that mean?"

"Nothing. Let's go to English."

Sheldon tried it again at lunch. He and Paul were sitting in the cafeteria at a long table of students, and the conversation was light when he suddenly burst out with:

"Hey, what does everybody think of our new president, Mike Otis?"

A long silence followed.

"Well, wasn't anybody paying attention? They announced today that he's president."

"What of?" asked Cindy Schwartz in between bites of her apple.

"Of you, of me, of all of us! He's student body president!"

"So?" inquired half a dozen voices.

"So nothing!" said Paul positively.

He was curious to see the effect of the presidency on Mike himself, so he looked forward to photography class with both anticipation and dread. But Mike was inscrutable as always. Mr. Willis was the only one in the room who seemed affected. Before beginning the lecture, he beamed at the back of the classroom and said, "I see we're honored to have the student body president himself in our little group."

This caused a slight hum, though Paul had expected more. Some of the students — Paul included — turned around to look, but Mike sat immobile and impassive, gazing ahead at points unknown. Paul had the feeling that Mike wouldn't have reacted if someone had tossed a live grenade behind his desk.

"Well, we've all brought our cameras today," said Mr. Willis, getting right to business.

"I didn't," chorused half the class.

"Well," said the teacher painfully, "I can still give my first lecture on basic composition."

Throughout the hour, even though the lesson proceeded as normal, Mr. Willis kept looking at the back of the class and shaking his head intermittently. Class was dismissed fifteen minutes early again, and Paul wondered if he would graduate from this course never having clicked the shutter of a camera.

After school, Sheldon said he felt like "hanging out" for a while, and Paul saw through it immediately.

"I know you," he accused. "You're looking for Mike Otis, aren't you?"

"Not especially," Sheldon replied casually, "but if we happen to run into him, I see no reason why we shouldn't congratulate him on his big win."

"Sheldon, you promised — "

"There he is now. What a coincidence."

"You're standing eight feet from his locker," Paul pointed out, but Sheldon had already run over to the new student body president. This presented Paul with a dilemma. Should he disassociate himself from whatever lunacy his friend had in mind (or hadn't even thought of yet?!), or in light of the fact that he was already in this thing and would be blamed no matter what, should he stick by Sheldon? That way he might be able to moderate Sheldon's plans, if not curtail them altogether. Taking a deep breath, he followed Sheldon.

"Hey, Mike," said Sheldon genially. "Congratulations!"

The beady eyes shifted from Sheldon to Paul and back again. "Why?"

"Student body president," said Sheldon. "That's great!"

Mike shrugged a vague assent and turned back to his locker.

"Well? What happens next?"

42

Mike looked faintly confused. "I'm going home."

"No, I mean what are you going to do as president? What's your first official act going to be?"

"Nothing."

"Nothing?" repeated Sheldon. "But then why did you become president?"

Mike shrugged again. "I don't follow a lot of that stuff."

"Well, are you going to meet with Mr. Gamble like he wants?"

"No."

Paul started to laugh and covered it up with a severe coughing spell. There was something to the old adage that you could lead a horse to water, but you couldn't necessarily make him drink. Mike Otis could become president of the galaxy and it still wouldn't impress him.

Mike closed his locker, gave Sheldon a self-conscious bye, and slouched off.

As soon as Mike was out of earshot, Paul allowed himself to laugh out loud. "Sheldon, you've got to stop teasing the poor guy like that. It's bad enough that you made him president. Now the least you can do is leave him alone."

Sheldon seemed abstracted. "If only we could get to know him better."

"We know him well enough to know that he doesn't want anybody to know him better!" snapped Paul. "*You* were the one who explained to me all about Don't Care High! Well, I don't think anything unpredictable has happened here except that you have lost your sense of perspective! Now let's forget this whole student body president thing and start living normal lives — under the circumstances!"

"You have no spirit of adventure," Sheldon complained.

I have no spirit of adventure, Paul thought as he lay in bed that night — and no imagination either. He could not for the life of him see the exquisite joy Sheldon seemed to derive from Mike Otis being student body president. What was the big deal? Yet last year, when some of his friends had put overalls on the school's statue of Sir David Kilgour on the day of the Queen's visit, he had stayed out of it, and had been unable to understand the great rejoicing when even Her Majesty had cracked a smile. And the year before that only peer pressure had forced him to participate in submitting the principal's name and photo in the "Sexiest Man in Saskatchewan Contest." And he had faked his laughter in the celebration when Mr. Phillips had won third prize.

What was wrong with him? Was it time to come to terms with the fact that he was — dare he say it? — dull?

A barrage of gunfire signified that the people in the next apartment were watching the late show.

Cover me! I'm going in there! shouted the hero masterfully.

Oh no, Steve! came the voice of the leading lady. *You'll never make it through the crossfire!*

You can't play it safe all the time, baby!

Sure, Steve, that's easy for you to say. You've read ahead in the script. They're going to aim fifty thousand cannons at you, and you aren't even going to get a flesh wound. You won't have a hair out of place. What do *you* know?

In the Paul Abrams version of the story, Steve sneaks out back and leaves town in the middle of the night. This hero hasn't read the script, and reserves the right to be a sniveling coward.

Paul could recall all of his friends expressing envy when he'd told them he was moving to New York. And what was he doing in the city? Being afraid of it. Letting the neighbors' TV blast him out of bed, crouching at his window like a Peeping Tom, watching the people in the building across the street, keeping his mouth shut while Auntie Nancy mixed into his mother's life and encouraged her to mix back. He had no right to look down on the Don't Care students. Exactly what was the difference between not caring and caring but not having the guts to do anything about it?

Back on the late show, they were awarding Steve a medal.

"Way to go, Steve," Paul muttered as he drifted off to sleep.

After school the next day, Sheldon delivered the crusher.

"We're going to follow Mike and see where he goes."

"What? Why?"

"We made him president," said Sheldon reasonably. "It's our duty to find out what kind of guy he is."

Paul's first impulse was to refuse flat out. Then he remembered Steve, the late show hero. It was not by refusing flat out that Steve had acquired the medal, not to mention the leading lady. What would Steve do? Refuse? Never. Then again, Steve didn't know Mike Otis.

"But we can't follow him. He has a car, remember?"

"That's to our advantage," Sheldon argued. "Have you ever seen the traffic in this part of town by three-thirty in the afternoon?"

Still muttering his complaints, Paul followed Sheldon to the bench near the narrow roadway which snaked in and around the high brick walls of the school and opened into the tiny, cramped parking lot nestled under the 22nd Street ramp. The two sat with studied nonchalance, waiting for their prey to drive out. It was ten minutes to four when the car appeared, a shiny black —

"What *is* that?" Paul gasped in awe.

"Wow!" breathed Sheldon. "He just gets cooler every day! Look at that car!"

The car looked like a German staff car from World War II, with a jet-black paint job that was lustrous and flawless. It seemed a little larger than a staff car, however, and just a little . . . different. Paul had always taken a keen interest in cars, but he was positive he'd never seen anything exactly like this before. Just when he was coming close to finding a category for it, he'd notice something that didn't fit, like the front grill, which was a work of art in itself; or the hood ornament, which seemed to depict the birth of Venus. Perhaps the main reason why the whole thing looked so alien was the fact that the man himself was hunched behind the steering wheel, a pair of mirrored sunglasses giving him the appearance of a World War I flying ace.

"Amazing!" exclaimed Sheldon without reservation.

He and Paul started on their way as the black behemoth eased into traffic. A woman in a red VW Rabbit, spying Mike in her rearview mirror, stuck her head out the window and gawked at the leviathan behind her, twice the size of her own vehicle.

Sheldon and Paul walked down the street, pacing themselves with the slow-moving traffic.

"Shel, I used to be into cars. I had books upon books upon books. I know every kind of car that ever existed, and that isn't one of them. Shel, what is that thing?"

"A masterpiece," said Sheldon. "Let's cross. He's turning left."

They had no trouble following the car. As Sheldon had predicted, traffic was slow and plodding. They lost sight of Mike only once, but a mad dash through a moving fleet of taxis got them caught up. About half a mile from the school, the great black automobile wheeled out of the line of traffic and disappeared down the tunnel of an underground parking garage.

Sheldon and Paul jogged up.

"No problem," said Sheldon. "We'll just wait for him to come out, and follow him home."

They found a newsstand a discreet distance away. Sheldon bought a paper, and they both hid behind it, keeping their eyes trained on the two exits. People came and went, but not Mike. After twenty minutes, they abandoned their position and circled the perimeter of the garage. There were no other doors.

"Strange," Sheldon commented.

"Maybe he's doing something with the car inside the garage," Paul suggested. "Like . . . uh . . . I don't know. Trying to figure out what the blasted thing is. Oh, let's just get out of here! We've seen him stare for twenty minutes at a locker; who knows how long he could spend with a whole garage? We could be here till midnight!"

"Yeah, I guess you're right," Sheldon admitted grudgingly. "But I know a place not far from here where they serve a slice of pizza that's not to be believed."

Paul made a face. "The last time you 'knew a place,' I was up all night with my insides on fire. And it's almost suppertime. My mother's pretty free with her lectures, you know, and the one about spoiling your supper is a classic I've heard all too often."

"We can't pass this up," Sheldon insisted. "The tomato sauce is so amazing that they've patented it under the name *Rocco*. Just one slice won't ruin your appetite. Come on."

". . . so I said to Nancy, 'You have money. If you want the dishwasher, buy it yourself and Harry won't say anything.' So she said to me, 'That's not enough. Harry has to want it, too.' Paul, you're not eating."

Paul shifted in his chair, and the tomato sauce

patented under the name *Rocco* resettled itself. "I'm just not very hungry tonight."

Mr. Abrams looked up from his plate. "I've got to apologize, son. I'm so busy lately that I hardly ever see you. But tell me, how's the new school going?"

Tears formed in Paul's eyes. His father thought they arose from the emotional content of the question. Paul knew they were from *Rocco*. "Well, it's not like Kilgour, Dad. It's kind of a weird school. You see, nobody cares. They all look like zombies, and nobody participates in class or asks any questions. It's not very good."

"Well," said his father, "are you sure a lot of that couldn't be explained away by the fact that it's in such a big city? Remember, we're not in the boonies anymore."

Paul winced. "We're not in the boonies anymore" had been a big catch-phrase for the move, designed to make New York more palatable, and put down Saskatoon. Paul had always thought Saskatoon was rather nice.

"Well, I don't know, Dad. Would you believe that they actually call the place Don't Care High?"

"I think that's just terrible," said Paul's mother. "Who was this Don Carey, anyway?"

Paul shrugged. "Oh, I don't know. I think he invented the sewer or something."

Mr. Abrams looked thoughtful. "No, the Romans did that."

"Maybe they forgot about it after the Romans," Paul said irritably, "and Don Carey revived the art."

"I don't think that's very funny," said his mother

primly. "And sewers certainly aren't table conversation."

"Sorry," said Paul. "I'm not feeling very well." Why bother these poor people with matters that were beyond their control in the first place? "Maybe things will get better," he added with a strange smile. "We have a new student body president."

4

May I have your attention, please. Here are today's announcements:

The Chess Club would like to list all those students who signed up this year: Seth Birenbaum. I am instructed to point out that, as soon as we have an opponent, we can forego the regular season games and the sudden-death elimination play-offs and go right to the finals for the championship trophy. There also appears to be a shortage of volunteers for the committee to go out and buy the championship trophy. Good luck, Seth.

Don Carey has again dropped out of the varsity football tournament due to heavy merging traffic on the Henry Hudson Parkway. This will come as no great shock to you, since the attendance at last week's tryouts was one — Coach Murphy.

Finally, Mr. Gamble would like to remind student body president, Mike Otis, that staff members are still willing and anxious to meet with him, although he has made no effort to see anyone thus far in his term of office.

That's all. Have a good day.

In chemistry class that day, Daphne Sylvester showed further signs of being alive. When Paul's Bunsen burner decided to go up in a pillar of flames, she actually demonstrated concern for his welfare by saying, "Okay?", which seemed to be a shortened version of "Are you okay?"

"I'm fine," breathed Paul, his hand still on the gas knob. "And my eyebrows will probably grow back."

Daphne didn't appear to appreciate this brave attempt at humor. Her attention, such as it was, had wandered back to Wayne-o, who was burning his name into the counter with pure, concentrated sulfuric acid. He was later caught at this, and Mr. Schmidt decided to mark him absent.

In geography, the first of the presentations on "The Industrial Giants" began. Samuel Wiscombe led off with a presentation on Japan. He walked to the front of the class and began to set up various maps, charts, and graphs, much to the delight of Mrs. Wolfe. He perched on the teacher's desk, took out a small stack of notes written on file cards, and began his introduction.

"This project deals with the economic factors affecting the direction of industry in China — "

"That's *Japan!*" shrieked Mrs. Wolfe.

Samuel shrugged. "Same difference."

When Mrs. Wolfe turned away from admonishing Samuel, she found her class stoic as always, with the exception of Sheldon and Paul, who were red-faced with laughter, tears running down their cheeks.

"You two! Out!"

The two boys couldn't even manage an apology. They got to their feet and stumbled out into the hall, still laughing.

"Well," gasped Sheldon, finally getting himself under control, "we seem to find ourselves with a two-hour lunch. So do we head for the cafeteria and dine on mildew, or do we check out the limitless vista of establishments our fair city has to offer?"

"I'll settle for the mildew," said Paul feelingly. "It's safer. Besides, I've got to study for my French test this afternoon."

Sheldon winced. "There's that ambition again. I thought you had it under control. Every now and then you just plain turn into a student. It's disgusting."

They had lunch, and Paul excused himself, saying he was heading for the library to study.

"Have you ever been in our library?" Sheldon called after him. "The lighting's so bad you can't see to read."

When Paul got to his locker, it was not, however, his French book he pulled out; it was his 35mm camera, which he slung over his shoulder. And his destination was not the library but the parking lot. Guilt for excluding Sheldon from this mission was not his major emotion — it was embarassment. But his embarassment did not outweigh his curiosity. Mike Otis's car had to be something, but what?

As he left the school building and stepped onto the broken pavement of the parking lot, he observed that, if an exiting vehicle ever jumped the guardrail on the 22nd Street ramp, it would drive right into Feldstein's stairwell. Then he saw Mike's car. It was bigger, shinier, and blacker than anything on the lot.

Camera at the ready, he examined the car from hood ornament to taillights. There were absolutely no identifying marks, with the exception of the Roman number *VIII* in tiny chrome letters on the back right-hand fender. Glancing furtively around him, he began to snap pictures of the car from every conceivable angle. This done, he returned to his locker, feeling self-conscious and not just a little foolish.

The next day, Sheldon and Paul entered the school to be greeted by a great hum in the corridor outside Feldstein's office. A group of students populated the hall in various relaxed postures, their eyes intent on a workman perched on a ladder. He had ripped out the old broken clock and was replacing it with a shiny new one.

"What's going on?" Paul asked the first face he took to be familiar. It was Peter Eversleigh.

Peter chewed on his breakfast licorice. "This seems to be a pretty conceptual deal to me. New clocks. This dude whom we are regarding has been installing these new clocks all over Don't Care." He added, "Care for some stick?"

"No, thanks. It's a little early for me."

"I'm amazed at this," commented Lucy LaPaz, one of the set of identical triplets in the school. "I've never seen anything new in this place."

Wayne-o was convinced that this was a symbolic gesture aimed at him. "They put those new clocks up so I should come on time," he mourned. "They want me there at the *beginning* of every class."

"No, that's not it," Sheldon said suddenly. "Mike Otis arranged for these new clocks."

Paul's breath caught in his throat.

"Who?" echoed a dozen voices.

"Mike Otis, our student body president. That was his very first demand. He saw what a disgrace it was that none of our clocks gave the same time, so he put some pressure on the school board, and look what happened."

Dick Oliver scratched his head. "I didn't know the student body president could . . . do things."

"Oh, he's got power, all right," said Sheldon. "What would a president do without power?"

Dick shrugged. "Nothing."

"Well," said Sheldon, despite frantic signaling from Paul, "maybe other presidents have no power but mark my words, when Mike Otis talks, people listen. These clocks are living proof. And that was pretty fast work."

An answering hum testified to the fact that many people had heard Sheldon's words. Paul grabbed his friend by the arm and hauled him away bodily from the group.

"What are you — sick?" he hissed angrily. "Why did you do that?"

Sheldon gave him an angelic smile. "I'm just helping out Mike. He'll have a much easier time leading the students once he has a few accomplishments under his belt."

"But this isn't his accomplishment! He'll probably be the last guy in the whole school even to notice that there are new clocks!"

"How could I resist?" said Sheldon dreamily. "Here was something just waiting to have credit taken for it. So I gave credit where credit was due."

"You're crazy," said Paul in disgust.

"Maybe," said Sheldon honestly. "But didn't you think that there was one brief moment, one tiny shining instant, when those people back there cared? Not much, I admit, but remember, this is Don't Care High." He shook his head violently. "Don't you see? In a world where students of this school can care about something, no one can tell what wonderful things could happen next. It . . . it enriches the experience of life."

Paul's face radiated deep distaste. "And what are you going to do with your enriched life when people start going up to Mike Otis and saying 'Thanks for the clocks' and he says 'What clocks?'"

"Mike'll probably just say 'You're welcome' anyway. I don't think he's much for getting to the bottom of things."

"Well, don't you think this whole thing is a little unfair to poor Mike?"

Sheldon nodded. "I've thought of that. We owe him a bit of an explanation. But, being a Don't Care student, he's hard to talk to in school. We'll let him in on the whole thing when we call him this afternoon."

"Call him? We don't have his number."

"Well," Sheldon admitted, "yes we do. You see, while you were studying in the library yesterday, I went to guidance to ask Mr. Morrison for Mike's phone number. But the office was empty. So I went over to the confidential files, pulled Mike's record, and photocopied it. I had it home with me last night. It makes for fascinating reading."

Paul was horrified. "That's not only immoral and unethical, it's probably illegal! This is disgusting! You're disgusting!" He paused and studied the floor. "What did it say?"

Sheldon beamed. "Just a lot of stuff about where he was born and the different schools he went to. His marks are nothing to scream about — mostly low seventies and a lot of comments like 'Michael could be an excellent student if only he'd try.' It almost reminds me of me."

"It doesn't say 'make of car' in there anywhere, does it?" asked Paul with some embarassment.

Sheldon shook his head. "No. But I did get his

phone number and address and anything else we would need to know. We can call him from your house after school today."

"Why not your house?" asked Paul.

"My father's hosting a big meeting this afternoon. They all collect airplane boarding passes, so they formed a society, and my Dad's vice-president. It seems some guy has dug up an old pass from Transatlantica's Flight 643, the only flight to go direct from Zurich to Cleveland, and they're coming from far and wide to look at it. Sometimes I wonder about my family. I'm crazy, and I'm still the sanest guy in the place."

The elevator doors opened on the thirty-third floor of Paul's building, and Sheldon and Paul found Mrs. Abrams standing there, car keys in hand.

"Oh, Paul. Thank goodness you're here. Hello, Simon."

"That's Sheldon, Mom."

"Yes, of course, dear. I'm in a terrible rush. I've got to go over to your Auntie Nancy's. Your cousin Cheryl sat in some tea."

"So?"

"She's in the hospital with first degree burns! Everyone's very upset, especially poor Nancy. I must run. I'm needed there. Oh, and your father won't be home for dinner tonight. I'm afraid you're on your own, Paul. This is an emergency." She dashed into the elevator which Sheldon had been holding open for her, the doors shut, and the car bore her away on her mission of mercy.

"Sat in some tea," Paul repeated, shaking his head as they entered the apartment. "And you say *your* family is crazy? What say we go over to your place and have a look at that boarding pass before the guy leaves?"

Sheldon smiled appreciatively. "We've got business." He opened up a notebook and produced his copy of Mike's file. "Here we go. Do you want me to do the talking?"

"Please do."

Sheldon dialed the number and sat listening, a puzzled frown coming over his face. He hung up, then handed the receiver to Paul. "Here. You try."

Obediently, Paul dialed.

"The number you have dialed is not in service. Please hang up and dial again."

Paul looked at Sheldon in surprise. "What do you make of that?"

"He must have changed his number over the summer and forgotten to register the new one with the school. But look, we have the address. Let's go over there."

"Aw, come on, Shel, couldn't we just forget about it for the time being?"

"No," said Sheldon positively. "We owe the guy an explanation."

"Well, if you could learn to keep your big mouth shut, we wouldn't owe him anything."

"One-oh-six Gordon Street, apartment eleven twenty-five," Sheldon read. "That's a short subway ride from here. Let's go."

One-oh-six Gordon Street was a small, modern apartment building set in the middle of very old row housing. It was an attractive red brick structure with wrought-iron balconies trimmed with flower boxes. Paul wondered why Auntie Nancy hadn't searched out such a place for his family instead of the chrome-and-gunmetal giant she had settled them into.

They walked into the building and headed straight for the elevator, which opened at the call button.

"Shel, are you sure we have to go through with this?"

"Yes, I'm sure. Now shut up and press eleven."

"There is no eleven."

"Don't be silly. There has to be. The guy lives in apartment eleven twenty-five."

"Well, there isn't."

Both boys stared. There were buttons for the basement, and floors one through ten, but no eleven.

"The numbering system must be different," Sheldon concluded. "We'll ask the superintendent."

The superintendent's office was on the main floor, and the super himself was a big burly man in a greasy undershirt. He was watching a *Gilligan's Island* rerun when the two boys entered the office.

"Yeah?"

"Excuse me," said Sheldon politely. "How can we find apartment eleven twenty-five?"

"With great difficulty," the man wisecracked in a deep booming voice. "It would be up on the roof with the pigeons. This is a ten-story building, kid."

"Oh . . . well, where can I find the Otis family?"

"There ain't no Otis family here, buster, unless they snuck in last night and didn't tell me."

"Well, they must have moved," Sheldon concluded. "Do you have a forwarding address?"

"I've been here twelve years, kid, and there ain't never been no Otis family. Now, go away. Ginger's going to sing."

Paul spoke up. "The fellow we're looking for is about my height, seventeen, long straight hair greased back, he always wears a big raincoat and sticks safety pins in the cuffs of his pants, and he drives a black . . . uh . . . car."

The superintendent stared at him, his expression a combination of malice and pity. "Look, I've never seen a guy like that in my life, and if I did, I'd call the cops. Now, leave me alone."

The boys left hurriedly, only to stand on the sidewalk staring back at the building.

"That's one-oh-six, all right," Sheldon confirmed. "And this is Gordon Street. I don't understand it."

"This is too weird," said Paul in exasperation. "He drives a car that isn't anything, his phone number is phony, and he lives on the eleventh floor of a ten-story building. And every day he drives home from school, goes into an underground parking lot, and never comes out. It's as though the guy doesn't even exist!"

Sheldon shook his head again. "I just don't understand it. But as long as we're on our own for dinner, it occurs to me that we're not too far from Omniburger, where they make the best burgers in town. And fries — oh, man! I'd sell my sister's cat to a tennis racket company just to inhale the aroma of those fries!"

"Sheldon — " began Paul warningly.

"We have to order the Megaburger. It's a whole pound of meat on an eight-inch bun. It comes with Ton-o'-Fries and Vat-o'-Coke. We can split it."

"Sheldon, this isn't another one of your deadly poison places, is it? I mean, there's no patent on these burgers, I hope?"

"Heck, no, this is gourmet junk food at its finest. Come on. Let's go."

Paul let himself into the empty apartment, clutching his midsection, where the Megaburger simmered, surrounded by his share of the Ton-o'-Fries. Passing the hall mirror, he looked at his green face. In the past two hours, he had taken in enough grease and oil to keep a fleet of taxis in perfect working order for six months. He switched on the radio in time to hear Flash Flood proclaim,

"Isn't it a beautiful evening in the greatest city in the world?"

"No!" Paul shouted. Mike Otis was on his mind, and fast becoming the only thing on his mind aside from his overtaxed digestive system. He sat down heavily at the kitchen table and noticed that Sheldon had left Mike's confidential file sitting there. Curiosity overcoming heartburn, he began to study it.

OTIS, MICHAEL
BORN: APRIL 1, 1968
PLACE: FINCH, OKLAHOMA

An odd feeling came over Paul, one which had nothing to do with the Ton-o'-Fries, and he all but ran to his room for the large family atlas.

"North Carolina, North Dakota, Ohio, Oklahoma . . . Finch . . . aha!" There *was* no Finch, Oklahoma. Paul was not surprised.

Replacing the atlas, he wandered to the window. Well, this certainly was a situation. Raincoat and safety pins notwithstanding, Mike Otis didn't seem to exist. Out of a school of twenty-six hundred students, Sheldon had picked at random the only one with no past and no present. As for the future, Paul could only shrug out the open window. It boggled the imagination.

A burst of flame caught his eye, and he squinted into a window of the building across the street. It was a fire-eater, getting in a little extra practice at home. Paul found it pretty mundane, actually, when compared to Mike Otis's uncanny ability to disappear off the face of the earth.

It was as though the fire-eater had guessed Paul's thoughts and was insulted, because he stuck his head out the window and blew a fireball at Paul. Involuntarily, Paul jumped back.

Flash Flood's voice reached him from the living room. "It's seven forty-six in the greatest city in the world. The late traffic is a mess in the tunnels, and the weather is going to be lousy. Face it, the world's too complicated to try and figure out tonight, so stay home and stay tuned to the old Double 9."

Paul smiled in spite of himself. Flash Flood was no dummy.

5

Rolling into the third week of school, a number of things changed. The weather went from insufferably hot to unseasonably cold, and naturally, the climate control system that governed the air inside Don Carey High School was taken completely by surprise. The school staff apparently gave up trying to meet with student body president Mike Otis, as he was no longer mentioned in morning announcements. And Paul Abrams became the first student ever to understand fully the system employed by the LaPaz triplets.

Lucy, Shirley, and Rose LaPaz, identical in every

way, were in Paul's math class, his second-to-last class of the day. Only one of the LaPazes was registered for the course, and therefore only one would attend any given math class. However, Paul had begun to notice he would be in class with a different LaPaz every day. They were quite open about their respective identities, and did not mind Paul's leading questions, but they would not reveal to anyone the secret and purpose of their system.

Through careful observation, though, Paul had worked it out. Each girl would receive her schedule of six courses, and would immediately request that she be changed out of any course she might share with a sister. Mr. Morrison, ecstatic over students showing an interest in the curriculum, would be only too happy to oblige. This left the sisters with a total of eighteen courses, through which they rotated in turn. Come exam time, there was a great pooling of information, and finals would be divided up, six apiece, each test to be written by the most capable in the subject.

"Wow!" exclaimed Sheldon when Paul let him in on his findings. "Ambition, you never cease to amaze me."

When they confronted Rose LaPaz with the theory, she seemed pleasantly surprised. "That's quite a piece of detective work."

"Oh, we never would have figured it out," said Sheldon modestly. "But Mike Otis knew it for a long time."

"Who?"

"Mike Otis, our student body president. He's unbeatable."

Rose looked impressed and went off to tell her sisters.

That was the way it was becoming with Sheldon, Paul observed, not without some trepidation. Mike Otis was terrific. Mike Otis was wonderful. Everything good that happened was entirely the work of Mike Otis, regardless of reality.

The part that really worried Paul was that Sheldon didn't seem to be joking anymore. He had apparently convinced himself that Mike was some kind of superman. It was getting to the point where talking with Sheldon on the subject of the new student body president was downright impossible.

"You know, Shel," Paul would say, "don't you think you're overdoing this whole Mike Otis thing a little? I mean, he's just a creepy little guy — "

"He's not creepy, he's just avant-garde, that's all. He's, let's say, the symbol for the nineties, so how can we, as eighties people, expect to judge him?"

"If weird is the way of the nineties, then I agree with you. I mean, I've got nothing against the guy, but he's strange. I've told you about how he doesn't exist."

"Oh, that," scoffed Sheldon. "A few mixed-up records. Mistakes like that happen every day. The guy is just too cool."

Paul shivered. He knew, for this week anyway, *everyone* at Don't Care High was too cool. In response to last week's heat wave, the janitors had managed to get the fans circulating cool air, just in time for the cold spell. So all the students wore thick sweaters and coats to class. All except the student body president, who continued to move about the school shrouded in his voluminous raincoat.

Sheldon took this to be one of Mike's many endearing qualities. "Look at the guy!" he crowed gleefully. "Nothing can make him change his habits! Not even the elements!"

> *May I have your attention, please. Here are the day's announcements.*
>
> *Due to the cold inside the school, the cafeteria staff requests me to tell you that there will be no fruit juice offered for sale today. There will, however, be snow cones available at the same price.*

Paul nudged Sheldon. "That guy's crazy! You can never tell whether you should believe him or not!"

"He was meant for the stage, not the desk," Sheldon whispered back.

> *On a somewhat less credible note, there is a program of restoration and repair planned for the school over the next couple of weeks. Consequently, there will be a number of workmen employed both in and around the building. We suggest that you steer clear of these people and let them get on with the job. That's all. Have a good day.*

Paul could tell from the wide smile of pleasure on Sheldon's face that his friend had big plans. He could see the wheels turning as Sheldon anticipated heaping credit on Mike Otis for each and every improvement made in the school during the weeks to come.

"I didn't know the student body president could do that kind of stuff," said Phil Gonzalez after listening to Sheldon explain how Mike Otis had singlehandedly arranged for the renovations to the school building.

"Of course he can," Sheldon assured him, "if you're lucky enough to get a guy like Mike Otis in office."

Wayne-o was impressed by Mike's reparations to the toilet facilities. "Good," he commented. "You see, I spend a lot of time in the can — not using it, but, you know, killing time between classes."

Rosalie Gladstone also took a particular interest in the washrooms. "Those new mirrors — you can see yourself in them!" She snapped her gum loudly. "I like to brush my hair a lot because I've got such great-looking hair when it's brushed right. The old mirrors are, like, foggy. I thought it was me."

"Well, you thank Mike Otis the next time you see him," Sheldon advised.

"Who?"

"The guy I just said got you the mirrors!"

"Oh, yeah. I guess so. I don't know."

Feldstein was skeptical. "I don't know if I go for all this change. You know — clocks that give the right time, clean washrooms, new lighting. You can't tell where it's going to end. Before you know it, they'll bring in the P.T.A., and then the staff'll start taking over unused lockers and giving them away for not so much as a donut. I like the old ways."

"Mike's working to make those great days even greater," Sheldon assured him.

"When I think of Mike Otis, I see my 200C's," said Feldstein sulkily. "But I've got to admit he's sharp. From the standpoint of someone who once tried to negotiate with Mike Otis, I have to say I feel sorry for the school board. Still, the guy is bad news. He ruined my retirement."

When sandblasting of the school's stone front began, Sheldon had a large audience. "Mike Otis did this!" he shouted over the din of the machinery and the sounds of the usual morning traffic jam. "He saw what a dump the school was, and went to work for us!"

"What are you talking about!" called someone. "Who's Mike Otis?"

"The student body president, you jerk!" exclaimed Wayne-o. "He's the guy who fixed up the can! Don't you know *anything*?"

Sheldon beamed. He was making progress.

By Friday, Mr. Willis's last period photography class had advanced to the enlarging stage. This was slightly behind schedule, as the teacher pointed out, for a number of reasons, not the least of which was that it was not possible to use chemicals at room temperature when the darkroom was fifty-seven degrees. Then there was Wayne-o's annoying habit of arriving late and turning on the lights in the darkroom to see if anyone was there. And the class seemed to be having an inordinate amount of trouble just remembering to bring cameras to school. In many cases, there were no photographs to enlarge.

Looking at his contact sheet, Paul was impressed to see that most of his shots had come out. He was gratified to note that the pictures of Mike's car were sharp and comprehensive. He intended to mail those to the world's foremost car experts in the hope that one of them could identify the vehicle.

Mr. Willis came by and gazed critically at Paul's work. "Not bad. I suggest you blow up — "

"Blow up?" came a worried voice from across the room.

"*Enlarge!*" snapped Mr. Willis. He turned back to Paul. "Do the one of the front view of the car."

Paul had not counted on this. "Uh . . . but what about this one of these buildings?" He did not much care for presenting his picture of Mike's car with Mike there. "I mean, the texture of the brick —"

"Boring," said Mr. Willis. "Do the car. That bizarre grill, the hood ornament, the whole shape — which junkyard did you find it in?"

"The school parking lot," Paul admitted in a low voice.

"Really?" remarked the teacher. "I wonder what it is."

By the end of the class, only three of the students had produced finished prints. Many others had been ruined when the print drying apparatus decided to commit suicide, and incinerated a large part of the class work.

"No harm done," Mr. Willis was saying as the janitor sprayed fire-extinguisher foam on the smoking machine. Paul noted that none of his classmates seemed perturbed in the least by the accident. Equipment failure was a common thing at Don't Care High.

"Just a minor incident," the teacher assured his bored class. "No problem. It'll be good as new tomorrow."

The janitor glanced into the smouldering machine and pronounced, "Yep, you can write this sucker off."

"Well," said Mr. Willis painfully, "we can still go back to the class and look at the prints we do have."

The first picture was entitled "Wayne-o's Mother." It portrayed a pleasant-looking woman holding a cake with oven mitts.

"That's my mother," Wayne-o explained, "and she's just taken a cake out of the oven. Chocolate. You can't tell because it's black and white."

The second picture was an extreme close-up shot of a crushed grapefruit.

"I call it 'Perseverance of Citrus,' " said Trudy Helfield blandly.

Mr. Willis was round-eyed. "Why?"

"I was taking a picture of this pushcart downtown, and some Toyota rammed right into it. What a mess. Have you ever seen a banana make contact with a brick wall at thirty miles an hour? Anyhow, this grapefruit's rolling down the street, dodging all the cars like it's going out of style, and I'm thinking, What courage! Bus comes out of nowhere — wow! This is all that's left." She pointed dramatically to the photograph.

Mr. Willis swallowed hard. "So? The title?"

Trudy shrugged. "My brother thought it up. He's a philosophy student."

Paul was last. "This is . . . um . . . a car . . . uh . . . taken from the front."

"And — ?" prompted Mr. Willis.

"Well . . . uh . . ." Paul drew a blank.

"That's my car," came an unmistakable monotone from the back of the class.

Paul tried to look surprised.

The teacher looked at the photograph and then at Mike. "Yes," he said, smiling strangely. "Of course it's your car. Quite impressive, too. What kind of car is it, Mike?"

Mike paused, then said, "A black one."

Mr. Willis sent everyone home early.

As Paul walked out the door of the photography class, he found himself staring into a cardboard sign which read:

SORRY FOR THE INCONVENIENCE
REPAIRS UNDER WAY
PLEASE BEAR WITH US
MIKE OTIS
STUDENT BODY PRESIDENT

He stared at the sign for an instant, then stepped forward quickly, shielding it from view with his body until Mike had walked out of the classroom and out of sight. Then he went to look for Sheldon.

His friend was not hard to locate. Paul simply followed the trail of signs until he came upon

Sheldon, happily affixing one to the stretch of wall outside the music room.

"Hey, check it out!" Sheldon greeted him. "What do you think?"

"I think you've gone completely and totally insane!" Paul seethed. "What happens when the teachers see these things?"

Sheldon shrugged. "What's wrong with them? Mike's just keeping the students aware of what's going on, and showing his concern for their inconvenience."

"Oh, *Mike* is, is he? I just had to throw myself in front of one of those things so your precious Mike wouldn't see it and hit the ceiling!"

"Mike's far too mellow to hit the ceiling," said Sheldon defensively.

"Not mellow — dead, maybe. Sheldon, these signs have Mike taking credit for all the school repairs! In writing!"

"I admit that they may *imply* that Mike's in charge of the improvements," said Sheldon, "but there's nothing the staff can object to. They're just nice little 'Pardon us' signs, that's all."

Paul sighed. "I counted seven of those stupid things on the way over here. How many did you make?"

Sheldon indicated his armload. "I didn't count. Around thirty, maybe. It's a big school. It won't take long to get the rest of them up now that you're here."

Paul shook his head to clear it. "What are you going to do for a whole weekend without any acclaim to heap on Mike Otis? What if, God forbid, some work is done over the weekend that you don't notice, and Mike has to go unthanked?"

"Look," said Sheldon, "I've been stuck at Don't Care High a lot longer than you have. I've put up with the decaying building, sweated in the heat, shivered in the cold, and hocked my life for a few cubic inches of locker space. But mostly I've put up with the people. I think there are a lot of nice guys who go to this school, but half the time you have to hold a mirror to their mouths to see if they're still breathing. If you go by their liveliness, most of the kids probably qualify as vegetation. Now, this year everything started to go right. I met someone who, despite his ambition, is a person I can talk to. And together we made Mike Otis student body president. At first it was just a joke because we could have made my little brother's gerbil president. But now I see we can do something. I'm not sure what it is, but I think I see that it's possible for the students of this school to be different than they are now, and that's something we have to try." He smiled engagingly. "At least you'll admit we don't have anything better to do."

Paul gazed at his friend with grudging admiration. If Sheldon wanted to go into politics, he certainly had the mouth for it.

That night, there was more high drama and adventure going on in the next apartment, where the late movie raged on as usual. It was impressive that, night after night, the neighbors managed to find a movie with the appropriate quota of gunfire, explosions, sirens, and hand-to-hand combat. Better still, why was the hero always named Steve? Yes. Another Steve was getting another medal, and another leading lady. Was there a rule that all dashing, high-action adventure types had to be named Steve? Or was this a series — the same Steve as last time (but a new leading lady!)? Even more instructive, this movie had a Paul in it. Paul was the sniveling coward who got no medal and no girl, but did get his thriving law office torched while he was inside, double-crossing Steve to save his own hide. Tough darts, Paul.

He crawled into bed and pulled the covers up around his ears. Tomorrow Sheldon was going to go back to school and resume his efforts to establish Mike Otis as the savior of Don't Care High. Hmmph. But Sheldon did have one point: Neither of them had anything better to do. After all, what did it hurt to tell everyone that Mike Otis was wonderful, so long as Mike Otis didn't mind? So what would it hurt to help Sheldon who, in a world of Feldsteins, Morrisons, Daphne Sylvesters, and Auntie Nancys, had befriended a lost soul from Saskatoon? It could even be fun. It was certainly better than sitting in a law office with no spirit of adventure, waiting for someone to throw a Molotov cocktail.

That settled it. Next week he would try to become one of the president's men.

6

The weather warmed up, and the rain began. Don Carey High School dripped. In some fourth floor rooms, the problem was so bad that classes had to be relocated to the basement, which seeped. Feldstein's stairwell had four inches of water, and the locker baron was forced to spend his office hours in hip boots. The halls became semi-swamp, and the ancient terrazzo floors were so slippery that one workman atop his stepladder slid fifteen feet before crashing heavily into the fire doors. He sustained a sprained ankle and multiple bruises.

It was this news that greeted Mr. Gamble upon

his arrival Monday morning, the rain and traffic already having grated on his nerves.

"The parking lot is a swimming pool!" he told Mrs. Carling as he took off his boots and wrung out the cuffs of his pants. "Some idiot parked a big black, gas-guzzling dinosaur in my space! I don't need to hear about accidents and floods. It's just like the school board to paint our walls when what we need is to have our roof fixed!"

"The injured man is in the nurse's office," the secretary informed him. "He's very upset. He wants to sue — "

"I'll see him." The vice-principal walked out of the office and stopped short. Directly facing him, bold as brass, was one of Sheldon's signs. " 'Mike Otis?' 'Sorry for the inconvenience?' What the — ?" He ripped it off the wall, opened the office door, and yelled, "Morrison!"

Mr. Morrison came over and examined the sign. "I know. They're all over the school."

"He takes credit for all the work we've been fighting for for years," growled Mr. Gamble.

"It is a little high-handed," Mr. Morrison admitted. "But it's a nice idea, don't you think? Certainly for a boy like Mike — "

"There's no way Otis made those signs. I know that boy!"

"Then who did?" asked one of the secretaries.

"How should I know?" raved Mr. Gamble. "Presumably the same troublemaker who nominated Otis in the first place!"

"Son-of-a-gun," commented Mrs. Carling.

"'Sorry for the inconvenience!'" snorted the vice-principal. "For two pins I'd go on that P.A. system, and then the *true* meaning of inconvenience — "

"You can't!" exclaimed one of the junior secretaries, aghast. "The boss would never let you make an announcement!"

"That's another thing wrong with this dump! *He* hides there in his office, leaving us up to our necks in work, not to mention water, but heaven help us if we try to touch that P.A. system, because it might take away from his morning vaudeville routines!" He shuddered. "I'll be in my office." He stormed inside and slammed the door.

May I have your attention, please. Here are the day's announcements:

Due to lack of interest, the Don Carey Alumni Association will not be meeting again this year. Therefore I am canceling the call for volunteers to serve on the decorating committee — not that there were any.

Unfortunately, the cafeteria will not be serving food today due to water leakage into the supply of dehydrated mashed potatoes. The dining area, however, should be shoveled out by noon.

Finally, Mr. Morrison urges me to remind you to keep selling those raffle tickets or else we will be unable to purchase a prize. That's all. Have a good day.

To begin his career as an Otis man, Paul decided to start off by watching Sheldon, the master, at work.

Sheldon started right after homeroom by telling a group of soggy Don't Care students he amassed in the slippery hallway that Mike Otis had anticipated this situation and pleaded with the school board to do something about it.

"Bureaucrats! They wouldn't listen! Mike begged them to fix the roof and waterproof the school before the rest of the work, but he just couldn't get through to them!"

"Mike — Mike — " repeated Cindy Schwartz in a puzzled tone. "Isn't he the guy who you said got the halls painted?"

"Exactly," said Sheldon, snapping his fingers in triumph.

"And he fixed the can, too," added Wayne-o.

"Why does he do all this stuff?" came a voice from the group.

"Why does he do it?" repeated Sheldon, leaping up onto a bench for height. "Because he *cares!*"

An enormous hum went up in the hall.

"Bad move, Shel," whispered Paul. "I think caring is even worse than having ambition."

"It had to be said sooner or later," Sheldon replied in a voice vaguely reminiscent of last night's Steve. "Let's go to class."

In English, Miss Vlorque was handing back Friday's test. As Sheldon and Paul entered the room, she had called Dick Oliver up to her desk to discuss his paper.

"Dick, you did very well, but one thing confuses me. Why did you write 'Cooking' under 'subject' in your exam booklet?"

Dick looked completely blank.

"This is English," Miss Vlorque went on. "Shakespeare."

"You're kidding!"

Miss Vlorque blew up. "How could anyone possibly mistake this for a cooking class? Do you see cooking equipment anywhere? Have we cooked anything?"

"Yeah, but I thought this was . . . you know . . . theory."

"If you didn't even know what course this was, how could you have done so well? You got a ninety-five!"

Dick shrugged. "I studied."

Miss Vlorque buried her face in her hands. "Tell me this isn't happening! This is a joke, right?"

Dick thought it over. "Do you think I could stay in this class for the rest of the term? I mean, cooking class has probably started without me, and I seem to be good at this."

"Do what you like!" she moaned. "Just go and sit down!"

"Man!" Dick muttered to Sheldon and Paul as he headed for his desk. "I should have known right off when there wasn't any stove that something was wrong. But, you know, you cut a few classes, come late a couple of times, maybe you don't pay attention so hot in the first place — it all gets by you. You know — Hamlet, omelet. It's all so similar."

Sheldon and Paul exchanged agonized glances.

"No sense staying here," said Sheldon in a strangled voice. "We'd only get kicked out anyway."

The two burst out laughing and ran for the door. They found a nice dry place to hide where they could chuckle themselves out. They had regained their collective composure in time to share Wayne-o's big entrance into English class about twenty minutes later.

Paul made his first stab into the world of politics in chemistry class. He looked way up into the exquisite countenance of Daphne Sylvester and said, "So what do you think of all the great things Mike Otis, our student body president, has been doing lately?"

"Who?"

"He's the guy who fixed the can," called Wayne-o from across the lab.

Another voice rang out. "Hey, someone told me today that that guy Mike cares."

A hum waxed and waned.

Paul turned triumphant eyes back to Daphne. She draped her gorgeous frame over the lab stool and motioned for him to begin the day's experiment.

Undaunted, Paul forged on. Working shoulder to shoulder with Sheldon, he helped spread the word of Mike Otis all through the halls of Don Carey High School. Even the most dubious and disinterested had to sit up and take notice when, on Wednesday, an emergency roofing crew arrived, just as Sheldon and Paul had predicted. In fact this was due to an area of roof which had caved in under the weight of water, completely demolishing Mr. Willis's fourth floor office. Sheldon called it "the school board giving in to Mike Otis's reasonable demands." Peter Eversleigh called it conceptual. Wayne-o called it another great achievement by the guy who fixed the can.

"Well," said Paul on Friday after school, "I don't know if all those Don't Care students appreciate Mike Otis, but I can sure say that by this time they've all heard about him."

The two boys sat in Sheldon's room listening to Flash Flood.

"Welcome to Day Five of the Universal Deluge. This is Flash Flood reporting that there are flash floods in various underpasses, subways, and basements. If you're on the road right now, you're not going to get home until midnight. Tonight's forecast is wet. It's four forty-five in the greatest city in the world, where nothing is dependable, and the only thing you can rely on is the fact that I will be here at Stereo 99 with all the music you're ever going to need."

Sheldon yawned hugely. "It's almost hard to believe — not only does Don't Care High have a president, but everybody knows his name. And he's doing things for the school."

"He isn't doing things for the school," Paul reminded him. "We're telling everybody he is. Keep at least a loose grip on reality, please."

"Even Wayne-o knows about Mike," marveled Sheldon. "Wayne-o! I was hoping we'd make an impression, but — *Wayne-o!*"

"When it trickles up to Daphne, I'll let you know,"

said Paul dryly. "I just can't help wondering what Mike thinks of all this."

Sheldon shrugged. "It probably hasn't reached him yet. He doesn't talk to anyone, you know. He may have seen one or two of the signs, but I'm sure he just ignored them. The big thing is what do we do next?"

Paul got a cold feeling in his stomach as the spirit of Steve deserted him. "What do you mean 'next'?"

"Fame is fleeting. Mike could be here today and gone tomorrow, and Don't Care High accelerates that process."

"Well, I don't see what we can do about it," said Paul. "Pretty soon we're going to run out of repairs and accomplishments. And we can't exactly take out an ad in the newspaper telling the world how wonderful Mike is."

Sheldon broke into a wide, toothy grin. "Ambition, you're a genius. Mike should be proud to have a man like you in his camp."

"What? A newspaper ad? That costs money!"

"Not in our own newspaper it wouldn't. You see, Don't Care High has a print shop — obviously out of use for some years now. That shop is there for student use, and what better use than a publication from Mike to his constituents?"

"Aw, Shel, we'd better think about that first. Making up stories is one thing; writing them down is another. I mean, if we have to go to the office to ask for the key to this shop, they're going to know the paper comes from us."

"It's an open shop," said Sheldon. "There's no

door. The only thing we have to worry about is being seen, and we'll figure some way around that. We'll arrange with Feldstein to get a few lockers nearby so it'll be a close stash before distribution."

Paul groaned. Feldstein again.

"We need a name," Sheldon continued. "How about *The Otis Report*? What do you think?"

"It'll look snappy on our expulsion papers," grumbled Paul.

"Most important, we need a picture. Mike, his face radiating honesty, industry, good will, and the ability to get things done. Something for the students to get behind and stay behind. Now they just have a name; they need a face to capture their trust."

"Just think for a minute of the particular face you're talking about," Paul interjected. "It *looks* like the face of someone who lives on the eleventh floor of a ten-story building. He looks like he comes from a nonexistent town, which he drove here from in a nonexistent car. He looks like he's *completely out of it!*"

"All the more reason why he should really catch on. Everyone in the school is completely out of it, too. Now look, he's in your photography class? Make him your next project."

Paul shook his head. "I'm really not sure about all this, Shel."

Sheldon grinned. "Of course you're sure. You're coeditor, aren't you? And staff photographer to boot. That's a lot of responsibility. Now let's start writing copy."

7

When the rain stopped, Mike Otis wasn't the only big story at Don't Care High. Feldstein, his authority being challenged for the first time this year, was on the warpath. Two freshman boys, unheeding of the locker baron's supremacy, had dared to saw off Feldstein's locks and replace them with their own, thereby taking unlawful possession of two lockers in the 800A's. Feldstein served them with fair warning, and they had responded by stealing and hiding the locker baron's chair.

In a rage, Feldstein extended his influence to the maximum, calling for hostility and inconvenience to rain down on the heads of the two transgressors. They were no longer allowed in the cafeteria, and all drinking fountains were closed to them. They were late for all classes, as access to their ill-gotten lockers was barred around the clock. And they were shunned like lepers by virtually all of the twenty-six hundred students.

Throughout this, Feldstein stood in his stairwell, arms crossed with grim determination.

When Sheldon and Paul went to see Feldstein on Monday, his chair had rematerialized, and the two transgressors stood before him, shame-faced and repentant.

"We were wrong, and we apologize," said the one on the right.

"We'll give you back the lockers," said his partner, "and we're willing to make it up to you."

"We'll do anything," added the first boy.

Feldstein's expression was solemn. He paused as the boy's words echoed in the upper stairwell, then reached into his pocket, produced a piece of paper, and began to unfold it.

"I have here a list of the Chinese food that I need right now. Make sure you get everything exactly the way it's written down. And I want you to know that, as far as I'm concerned, absolutely nothing happened between us."

"Gee, thanks, Feldstein! We'll get it right away!" The two boys sprinted out of the building.

Sheldon and Paul approached the locker baron.

"Hi, Feldstein," said Sheldon. "I see you've done it again. Congratulations."

Feldstein nodded sadly. "Business is business,

but this — " he gestured in the direction in which the two freshmen had departed " — is just a couple of kids who don't know what they're getting into. The locker game sure has changed. Two years ago, the great insurrections of Slim Kroy and The Combo. The year before that, I was the young upstart, forcing Fitzpatrick completely out of the A's and establishing my first stronghold. Those were the days." He sighed. "You've got to do a lot of dirty things in this business. So what can I do for you today, man?"

"We need two lockers as close to the print shop as possible."

Feldstein brightened. "No sooner said than done. 468 and 469D, right across. Why don't you take 470, too? On me."

"You're a prince, Feldstein," said Sheldon, pleased.

"Yeah, thanks, Feldstein," added Paul.

"Don't mention it, man."

Photography class continued to have its problems. Mr. Willis, who now had no office and no print dryer, continued valiantly to teach and refused to give up precious darkroom time. Replacing the dryer was an electric fan he had unabashedly swiped from Mr. Gamble's office. He urged all students to bring electric hair dryers to class, but only he and Paul had remembered to do so. This inadequate resource was cut in half when Mr. Willis' dryer was recalled by the manufacturer.

That Wednesday, Paul was confronted with the problem of a portrait shot of Mike Otis. This,

Sheldon was telling him, was holding up the first edition of *The Otis Report*, which was otherwise ready to go to press.

As the class waited for Mr. Willis to arrive, Paul made an elaborate show of announcing that his camera was broken. Putting his eye to the viewer, he wheeled around, saying, "See what you can make of this." Aiming the camera directly at Mike, he snapped a picture. "Hey, what do you know — it's fixed. Thanks, Mike."

"You're welcome."

He waited until school was over to develop the picture. He and Sheldon stood over the developing tray, watching with anticipation as the image grew more distinct.

Sheldon crowed with delight. "Excellent, Ambition! You've got talent!"

Paul smiled proudly. It was a head-and-shoulders shot of the student body president, and rather a good likeness. He had apparently caught Mike in a state of slight surprise, but this was a plus, as the usually heavy eyelids were almost completely open, and the beady eyes looked faintly alert. The sleek head was cocked slightly to one side, and the collar of the raincoat was up, looking like a vase out of which was growing Mike's face.

"It looks great," Sheldon said. "Obviously, he's every inch a leader. How did you get the eyes so open? I can't see any toothpicks."

"Just lucky, I guess. How many of these do you need?"

"A smaller one for the paper," Sheldon replied. "But hang onto that negative. It's beautiful."

* * *

The next day, Sheldon and Paul arrived at school early and headed directly for the print shop. Sheldon brought along a huge bed sheet, which he hung in the entrance to the shop alcove. To this, Paul affixed a sign reading MEN AT WORK, which the boys had pillaged from an area of wet paint near the office. Paul tried out the new lockers to check that the combinations worked and that they were clean and clear and ready to receive material. Then he stood guard as Sheldon began production, trying to look nonchalant as the roar and screech of seldom-used machinery emanated from behind the bed sheet. There was virtually no one around, and Paul felt comfortable running the first bundles of the finished product over to the lockers for storage.

Then unforeseen circumstances arose. At less than two hundred copies in print, Sheldon ran out of paper, and Paul was forced to raid a nearby storeroom, which was fortunately unlocked. His heart pounding in his ears, he grabbed paper packages of all sizes in the hope that one of them would fit the printer. Sheldon pronounced the operation saved, and Paul went outside to have a minor breakdown of sheer relief.

As time progressed, the halls began to fill with students, but no one was interested in the activity behind the sheet or the nature of Paul's numerous shipments from print shop to lockers. Paul lost count of the print run at eight hundred, but Sheldon was just getting started. Production went on right up until homeroom, when Sheldon and Paul locked up their fifteen hundred copies and headed for Mr. Morrison's class, a quiet environment in which they could rest and contemplate distribution.

Mr. Morrison was panicking about his raffle tickets, pleading with his disinterested students to get out there and sell, sell, sell. Sheldon and Paul took seats at the back of the class and settled down to listen to the tirade. Paul noticed that, while they were supposed to be discussing the distribution of *The Otis Report*, Sheldon was silently scanning one of the fliers, his expression growing increasingly solemn. By the end of the announcements, he was positively pale.

"You know," said Sheldon as the class was dismissed, "I don't think it would be such a good idea if any of the teachers knew it was us handing out those papers. For example, I don't think the staff is going to appreciate the part where we say that there hasn't been a single improvement this year that wasn't directly attributable to Mike."

Paul looked disgusted. "Well, I told you on Sunday when you wrote that drivel — "

"And when we quote that school board member we made up," Sheldon went on, "and Mike's telephone call from the mayor — oh, man! Remember the part where we said that, if Mike had been around, they never would have built the 22nd Street ramp? I think we called the staff and school board 'ineffectual.' "

"*You* called them ineffectual! *I* tried to talk you out of it!"

"Gee, maybe it was bending the truth too much to say that Mike was invited to be keynote speaker at the Student Government Conference in Dallas."

"I'd say so," Paul agreed sarcastically, "especially since the only thing we can really verify is the fact that there is a place called Dallas. But that's not the best part. The real crusher is when you talk about Mike's future plans to ride roughshod over everyone to make Don't Care High a student paradise. I believe the actual wording went something like 'whipping butts into shape.' "

Sheldon nodded. "If it's taken the wrong way, the staff could get pretty upset about that. We'll have to change our way of thinking a little."

"Change the paper?" asked Paul.

"Change the mode of distribution," Sheldon corrected. "It's all a matter of superior speed and a degree of camouflage."

"Superior speed?" Paul repeated.

The smile had returned to Sheldon's face. "How are you on roller skates?"

Friday was a cool, crisp day, the first day of the school year when the atmosphere inside Don Carey High School was comfortable. As the homeroom ended, students poured out into the halls to begin the long loiter that preceded first period.

This particular Friday, however, the normal hum of conversation and clang of lockers on the second floor was interrupted when the heavy doors at the far end of the hall were flung open dramatically to reveal two masked men.

With a cry of "*Now!*" the two figures, wearing ski masks and roller skates, and each carrying a huge bundle of newspapers, began to roll through the corridor, bestowing papers left and right.

"*Otis Report*! Get your *Otis Report*!"

"News from our president! Free!"

Paul sped down the hall, strewing papers wherever he saw people. Luckily, he was the former Kilgour High School roller skating champion, and this operation was a breeze for him. He was stepping deftly around students, weaving his way down the long hall. "Words from Mike! Words from the president!" Expertly, he spun around, knocked open the stairwell doors with a heavy hip-check, and ran lightly up to the third level to start the process all over again.

Sheldon, however, was having a harder time. He had grossly overestimated his own roller skating ability, and was careening around the hall at breakneck speed, slamming into lockers and students. He allowed his distribution to be governed by his own inability to hang onto his whole batch of papers and stay upright. Hurtling toward the end of the hall, only a last minute stiff-arm saved him from opening the heavy fire door with his nose, and he part-skated, part-hopped, and part-fell down the stairs. He landed only inches from Feldstein, who was digging into a stack of pancakes and syrup.

"Vermont maple syrup," the locker baron said, shaking his head. "I asked for Quebec."

Sheldon tossed a paper at Feldstein's feet and scrambled out onto the first floor.

Paul, meanwhile, was enjoying himself no end. Just delivering the papers was not enough for him anymore, and he was executing spins, dips, and pirouettes, earning such comments as, "So what?"

from the students. But the papers were *going*. He and Sheldon had talked up Mike Otis so much that the blasé Don't Care students were receiving *The Otis Report* with something approaching interest. It was the picture, Paul decided, that was striking chords of recognition. He could hear remarks such as, "Hey, I know that guy," and "That's the guy with the safety pins in his pants," as he danced gracefully along the corridor.

On the fourth floor, he found himself handing a copy into the hands of the student body president himself, and decided to try a little speed-skating, omitting his usual pitch. He did risk a backwards glance, however, impressing on his mind — possibly for life — the image of that face, staring at that face, which was undoubtedly staring back, and so on.

It was a feeling of freedom Paul hadn't experienced for years, rocketing through the drabness that was Don't Care High, yet removed from it all by a few thousand stitches of wool and eight wheels that gave him the ability to fly. Like this he could go where he pleased, even by the office if he so chose, for the power was his.

He tossed his remaining few papers into the crowded stairwell, shouted a final, "Get your *Otis Report*!" and worked up a head of steam for his grand finale into the bathroom that was serving as home base.

Paul could have avoided any stationary or smoothly moving target, but an erratically-flailing, high-speed, out-of-control Sheldon was beyond his expertise. They met head-on with a resounding crunch, and crumpled together through the bathroom door.

When the stars cleared from Paul's vision, he saw the battered Sheldon lying beside him, exhausted, on the tiles. Sheldon ripped off the ski mask, grinned awkwardly through partly swollen lips, and gasped, "A success!" before collapsing completely on the floor.

At the beginning of fifth period, Mike Otis was called to see Mr. Gamble. Sheldon and Paul, feeling responsible, cut class and went to hang around the outer office. When they found themselves on the receiving end of too many stares from the secretaries, they dropped in to the nearby guidance room, to the great shock and even greater joy of Mr. Morrison. To kill time, they allowed themselves to be coaxed into filling out career interest questionnaires, while keeping a sharp eye on the door in case Mike passed by. Apparently, though, Mike was either out of the building at the time of the call, or simply not receptive to paging.

"Maybe he thinks they're talking about another Mike Otis," suggested Sheldon as the two were walking to sixth period class.

The call went out again in sixth, but was apparently unanswered because, in photography, Mr. Gamble himself appeared at the door.

"Is Mike Otis here?"

"In a manner of speaking," sighed Mr. Willis, who was having his usual hard time getting the class under way.

Mike surrendered himself in characteristically

passive fashion, and was borne off to the office. Paul was overcome with guilt.

After class, he and Sheldon sought out Mike at his locker.

"Hey, Mike, what's new?" called Sheldon.

Mike gave them a quizzical look. "Nothing."

"Nothing," repeated Paul, nodding. In Mike Otis language, what did that mean? "Why did Gamble want you?" he blurted.

"There are a lot of things at this school I don't understand."

Sheldon and Paul stood there, waiting for the elaboration that would not come. Mike reached into his locker, produced a small polishing cloth, and dusted off the toes of his black dress shoes. He checked the security of the safety pins holding his cuffs and closed the locker door. He turned to leave and paused, perhaps pondering what to do with Sheldon and Paul.

"I guess you're going home now," said Paul lamely.

Mike nodded and headed for the stairwell.

"See you Monday?" Paul called after him anxiously.

Mike stopped and looked over his shoulder. "Sure." Then he disappeared down the stairs.

Paul exhaled. "He didn't get expelled! What a relief!" He wiped his forehead. "Oh, let's get a Coke! I'm buying!"

All the way to the deli, Sheldon kept up a steady stream of chatter in praise of Mike Otis. "Can you believe that guy? He's too cool for words! Gamble tears him out of class and probably chews him out for something that isn't his fault, and he says 'There are a lot of things at this school I don't understand.' What a philosopher! What a poet!"

"Calm down, Shel. People will think you're nuts."

"I mean, he's got life right where he wants it! Picture this: It's the battle of Waterloo, and Napoleon's forces are in ruins. Wellington demands that the French surrender, and Napoleon says, 'There are a lot of things in this war I don't understand.'"

"I don't see the connection."

"It'll come to you," Sheldon promised. "But when we picked Mike to be student body president, we picked a great man. I can't wait till next week when *The Otis Report* will have had a chance to sink in."

At three o'clock in the morning, Paul was awakened from a deep sleep by the persistent shaking of his shoulders. He sat up to find his mother standing over him.

"Wake up, Paul."

Paul rubbed his eyes. "What's the matter?"

"Your cousins Cheryl and Lisa are here."

Paul looked at his clock radio. "It's after three. Why can't they come visiting at a decent hour?"

"Paul, don't be uncooperative!" his mother admonished him. "Poor Auntie Nancy! Fluffy got sprayed by a skunk."

"Fluffy," Paul repeated dazedly. There was another sore point. Other people loved their dogs; Auntie Nancy was absurd about Fluffy. From years back, he could recall his aunt telling him, "Fluffy is not a dog. She's a little girl with long ears and a fur coat."

Paul yawned. "Why are you waking me up to tell me about this tragedy?"

"Well, you see, Fluffy went in the house, and now everything smells just terrible. The poor girls couldn't sleep, so they phoned and asked if they could come here."

"And you said sure," Paul sighed wearily. "Is Auntie Nancy here, too?"

"Oh no. She's at home with Fluffy."

Paul nodded sagely. "The captain stays with the stinking ship."

"Don't be insensitive, young man. Now, come on. Out of bed. I told Cheryl and Lisa that you'd be happy to sleep on the couch so they could have your room until things are back to normal at their house."

"Tell them I was misquoted," muttered Paul sourly.

But in the end, Paul had to make do in the den while his cousins, smelling faintly of skunk, took possession of his room, which was, Paul decided, true to the direction his life was taking. The Steves of this world may be masters of their own fate, but Paul Abrams goes where he's pushed.

8

The fumigation of Auntie Nancy's house and decontamination of its resident canine took all weekend, and Paul was forced to spend Friday, Saturday, and Sunday nights in the den. He did not sleep well, as the couch seemed to have several sizeable lumps which, for some reason, could not be found when his mother lay down to check out his complaints. Paul, in his sleepless frenzy, kept imagining large, beetlelike creatures crawling around below his body.

The small shift in location gave him a whole new angle from which to watch the apartment building across the street. The poker game had reconvened, but he could barely see it, although from this new perspective he discovered Rabbit Man. Rabbit Man lived at the corner of the building on about the thirty-fifth floor level, and every night he dressed himself in a bunny suit, sat in the window, and ate carrots. The first night, Paul had thought the man was on his way to a costume party; now he didn't know what to think.

Then there was the couple in the apartment adjoining the Abrams'. The elderly pair who, according to Paul's mother, "have been married forty-three years and have the most wonderful relationship," came to blows that weekend, hurling abuse and crockery at one another. Although not as instructive as the continuing adventures of Steve on the apartment's other border, they were much more interesting, and a lot louder.

To make matters worse, Sheldon and his family were away for a long weekend attending a boarding pass convention at a resort hotel in the Catskills. They were not scheduled to return home until Monday evening. This forced Paul to spend a lot of time at home, where he had to listen to the infernal beeping of the telephone with forwarded calls for his two cousins. In keeping with their eternal diets, there was cottage cheese at every meal, and Paul suffered from perpetual nausea Saturday and most of Sunday. He found himself thinking nostalgically of the tomato sauce patented under the name *Rocco*. All weekend he listened with a hopeful heart to bulletins on the progress of the tomato juice baths at Auntie Nancy's house.

So it was an exhausted and supremely overtaxed Paul who presented himself for school on Monday morning. The last thing he needed in this world, he reflected, was more aggravation.

Mr. Gamble and Mr. Morrison arrived at the office at the same time, each with *The Otis Report* on his mind. Mr. Gamble was in a state of outrage, roaring, "Otis doesn't have the slightest idea what's going on here! You can't even be sure whether he really knows he's president! This lunacy has got to stop!"

Mr. Morrison was in a quandary. Yes, *The Otis Report* was full of exaggerations and outright lies, but it was also a show of initiative — the first he had witnessed since his arrival at Don Carey. But if this effort wasn't attributable to Mike, then whose work was it? Who was showing this potential that, with proper nurturing, could turn into — dare he think it — school spirit?

"Son-of-a-gun," was Mrs. Carling's opinion.

"Furthermore, I want to make the announcement personally," Mr. Gamble raged. "I don't want our great leader to interpret this as some big joke. It's a hoax and it must be exposed and ended! And this time I'm not backing down!"

A hush fell as Mr. Gamble strode purposefully into the principal's office. One of the younger secretaries covered her eyes.

The regular bassoon voice came through the P.A. system that morning.

> *May I have your attention, please. Just a couple of announcements.*

We have a complaint from police that our students are straggling across the street in front of oncoming traffic, causing great inconvenience to motorists and danger to themselves. I will at this point reiterate that bit of sage advice which I am sure all of you have at one time or another had bestowed upon you. Please look both ways before you cross the street.

Oh yes, and this, according to Mr. Gamble, is important. For a number of reasons, Mike Otis will no longer be allowed to hold the office of student body president.

That's all. Have a good day.

A hum went up throughout the school. Paul felt himself suffused with rage. Instinctively, he looked around for Sheldon before remembering that his friend would not be in school until tomorrow.

The door opened and Wayne-o breezed in, his face mirroring perplexity instead of its usual blankness. "Hey, Mr. Morrison, did I just hear that they're not going to let Mike Otis be president anymore?"

"Yes," said Mr. Morrison uncomfortably. "The staff feels that Mike . . . uh . . . doesn't really have the support of the students."

Wayne-o looked confused. "*I* support him."

That was all Paul needed. He leaped to his feet. "Me, too! We all support Mike Otis, right?"

There was a thoughtful hum. As Paul scanned

his classmates, he saw vaguely surprised looks on their faces, as though the question had caught them off guard.

Dan Wilburforce verbalized what they all seemed to be thinking. "Well, I've never really thought about it much, but now that you mention it, I guess I do support Mike Otis. After all, he did do all those things for the school."

"He got the halls painted."

"He got the roof repaired."

"He fixed the can!" added Wayne-o breathlessly.

"Wait a minute," said Mr. Morrison. "Who told you all these things?"

There was silence for a moment, so Paul yelled, "Everybody knows it! It's all over the school!" And there was general agreement.

"And it was in the paper," Wayne-o added earnestly.

Mr. Morrison tried to choose his words carefully. "What would you say if I told you that Mike knows nothing about that paper and did none of those things?"

"But you're a teacher!" blurted one of the LaPaz triplets. "You have to say that!"

Paul spoke again. "They're trying to take away our duly-elected president!" As the words "duly-elected" passed through his lips, he went a little red and sat down.

"Besides," said Wayne-o, "It has to be Mike's paper. His picture's on it. And it's all about him."

Mr. Morrison gawked. "You *read* it?"

"Of course I read it," said Wayne-o, almost belligerently. "Okay, so I don't read a whole lot. But when the guy who fixed the can takes the time to publish a newspaper to keep me informed, I read it."

Mr. Morrison sat down at his desk, overcome by his homeroom's reaction. "All right, everybody. Go to class."

And suddenly Paul was on his feet again. "But if you support Mike, tell your friends about it! We can't let this snow-job go through! Remember, when we needed it, Mike was there to fight for us!"

The class dispersed, humming.

Paul went through his day as though in a coma, hardly understanding his own reaction. Classes were a blur. He felt great anger over Mike's dismissal, even though he was fully conscious of the fact that President Otis had sprung from the diabolical imagination of Sheldon Pryor. Yet when he saw a discarded and trampled copy of *The Otis Report*, he felt a rush of emotion and outrage that almost alarmed him. Mike's humble beginnings were unimportant now. He *was* the president. They couldn't impeach him. It was not fair.

When he arrived in photography class and saw Mike, it was all he could do to keep from running up and embracing the deposed leader. He did say, "Raw deal this morning, Mike, but the war's not over yet," and received a confused stare in reply.

A murmur went up in the room, and Paul could make out a few "That's him" and "That's Mike Otis."

Twenty minutes later, when the class was already under way and Wayne-o was making his entrance, the latecomer walked straight to Mike's desk, clapped a friendly hand onto his shoulder, and announced, "Hang in there, Mike. We're with you all the way."

Poor Mr. Willis just stood there, the progress of his chalk arrested halfway through the diagram of a camera. He stared in amazement as all his students turned to Mike Otis and offered murmured words of comfort and support.

After school, Paul went home and took possession of the phone. He was grateful that Cheryl and Lisa had been able to return home, but in his fervor, even this blessed event seemed unimportant. He called the Pryor house every fifteen minutes, finally reaching Sheldon on the fifth try.

"Shel, we have to meet. It's an emergency."

"What's up?"

"Don't Care High threw Mike Otis out of office."

There was a pause, then, "I'll be right over."

So urgent was the situation that the boys passed up their customary snack and did not even consider the radio. Sitting in Paul's room with the door closed, Paul outlined the events of the day while Sheldon listened gravely.

"Well, obviously we have to do something," said Sheldon. "But we *are* only two guys against the whole staff."

"No we're not!" said Paul vehemently. "I watched an entire class stop right in the middle so the students — Don't Care Students — could give Mike a vote of confidence. Our whole homeroom came out in Mike's favor. Wayne-o said, and I quote, 'I support him.' "

"That's incredible!" Sheldon marveled.

"All that being true," Paul went on, "they're still not the kind of people who get excited at the drop of a hat. They have to be told about Mike. They have to have a chance to think about it. It's not that they don't care; it's that they never think about it. Once they do, they're on our side."

Sheldon looked at Paul almost proudly. "You're really worked up about this, aren't you?"

Paul grinned in embarrassment. "You had to be there, Shel. You had to hear Mr. What's-his-name say that Mike couldn't be president anymore. I know it sounds funny, but it was like a kick in the ribs."

"If we can pull this off," said Sheldon, "it'll be the most amazing thing in the history of the world! We'll build it up so that everybody thinks that kicking Mike out of office was not only an offense against Mike, but twenty-six hundred individual slaps in the face. We'll demand that he be reinstated. "But," he added with a dazzling smile, "not before we have everybody's support. Because if we're singled out as the guys who started the whole thing, we're both instantly dead."

Step One, according to Sheldon, was The Face.

"We have to familiarize all the kids with Mike's face. It will give them something human to relate to."

On Tuesday afternoon, Mr. Willis's entire photography class, with the exception of Mike himself, stayed after school to do extra work in the darkroom. The result: one hundred gleaming eight-by-ten glossies of the beleaguered president, and an

105

agreement for a repeat performance the next day and subsequent days if necessary.

"We won't stop," Sheldon vowed, "until the teachers at this school are seeing Mike's face in their sleep!" His accomplices all nodded enthusiastically.

As the days went by, the word spread. Along with the appearance of countless photographs of Mike Otis peering off every wall, students were talking among themselves and finding, in an increasing ground swell of surprise, that they had an opinion on the subject. They were angry. No one could recall having voted for Mike Otis, but all assumed his position to be legitimate. Everyone sensed the growth of his support. The situation was simple. He had fought for the students, and for this he had been cast out.

"It's our responsibility to fight for Mike the way he fought for us!" Sheldon harangued an ardent cafeteria crowd.

"Yeah!" shouted a dozen voices.

"Yeah!" agreed still more.

"*Yeah*!" repeated everyone, until the single syllable grew into what would go down in history as the first cheer ever to come from a roomful of Don't Care students.

Paul produced a sheaf of photographs and jumped up onto the table that Sheldon was standing on. "If you're with Mike, show it! Display his picture!" He hurled the pictures out into the sea of eager hands.

Art classes became exclusively devoted to the manufacture of "We Want Mike Back" posters, which began to appear all over the school. All wood and metal shop projects were shelved in favor of the production of Mike Otis billboards and large ornamental M.O. initials. The school band set to work composing a Mike Otis anthem, which included a five-minute tuba solo played by one-time locker baron Slim Kroy. The anthem was never completed, but the tuba solo lived on. It sounded like a cross between "Old McDonald had a Farm," and "I Can't Get No Satisfaction," oompahed out at double-speed by Slim who, at two hundred fifty pounds, had the wind for it. It was quite catchy, and many of the students took to humming it under their breath. The picture of the burly Slim holding his tuba went on to become synonymous with Mike's quest to regain power.

Strangest of all, the students of Don't Care High, renowned for their consummate lack of interest in everything, had almost overnight blossomed into an energetic gang of political zealots.

Phil Gonzalez, whose former greatest achievement was the eleven-and-a-half-foot scratch he had put on his father's Coupe de Ville last Christmas, suddenly commandeered his home economics class. Unbeknownst to the teacher, he was leading his fellow students in the sewing of an enormous Mike Otis flag. The background was a basic blue, which coincidentally matched the color of some curtains missing from the teachers' lounge. On it was a huge white *O*, skewered by a giant silver safety pin. Sheldon had liked it so much that he had photocopied a hundred miniature versions of Phil's original design and put them into circulation with the already awesome amount of paper that was being passed around on behalf of the deposed president.

Cindy Schwartz, on the other hand, was participating on more of a creative level. Her big achievement was the coining of the phrase "I Like Mike." It caught on like wildfire, and began to appear on posters, banners, and blackboards throughout the school. Cindy invested the money to have a T-shirt made with her slogan, and also wrote it in brass studs on the back of her genuine vintage 1973 jean jacket.

Rosalie Gladstone was the maker of the campaign's largest poster, which consisted of no fewer than 208 pieces of construction paper. Naturally, there was no room for it on the already-cluttered walls inside the school, so she displayed it in the parking lot, protecting it from the wind by parking her Volkswagen on it.

Her effort inspired Dick Oliver to come up with the campaign's longest poster, which was eighteen inches high and 175 feet long, and used the word "Mike" thirty-five times. Dick strung this outside across the front of the building, where it would ultimately be shredded by the wind.

There was also a valiant attempt at the most voluminous poster, but the three-dimensional monstrosity collapsed to the floor while its creators were assembling it in the hall of the math wing.

One afternoon, Peter Eversleigh, while staring at a wall plastered with eight-by-ten glossies of Mike, became overwhelmed with the conceptuality of the situation, and began a rampage through the school halls, yelling at the top of his lungs to anyone who would listen, "*Mike Otis is our main dude!*" This finally ended on the fourth floor, where Peter collapsed with exhaustion, greatly in need of licorice.

A political science class burst into a violent shouting match after Dan Wilburforce suddenly blurted out, "How can you sit there and talk about democracy when Mike Otis was booted out of office even though all the students love him?"

Coincidentally, all the planned repairs to the school were over by that week. Sheldon pounced on this mercilessly.

"The minute Mike was gone, the school board stopped all its improvements to our school!" he howled at a cheering mob packed into a little-used fourth floor hall. "I think it's obvious that they got rid of Mike because he was *too effective!*"

Mike Otis was noticing changes in his life. His photograph was appearing all over the school along with posters and banners that screamed his name. A lesser man would have wondered why; Mike simply accepted it all as one of the things at this school that he didn't understand.

When he walked through the halls, students would come up to him, pat him on the back, and ask to shake his hand, saying things like, "You're the greatest, Mike," and "Hang in there, guy." Cafereria lincs would melt away so he wouldn't have to wait, and there were always students offering to carry his tray to a vacant table.

Once he happened upon one of Sheldon's rallies, and a few people at the rear recognized him. In an instant, he was swamped by a well-wishing mob, and forced to scribble his name on their countless photos.

Wayne-o had taken to trying to introduce Mike to all his friends. Mike was finding himself on the receiving end of almost incredible amounts of praise and gratitude.

"Mike, your courage is an inspiration to us all!" said Shirley LaPaz without reservation.

"I didn't do anything," said Mike in his usual dull tone, since a reply seemed to be called for. "I didn't do anything" was also Mike's reply to the group of well-wishers who mobbed his car on several mornings. "I didn't do anything," he told Wayne-o honestly on the subject of his fixing of the Don't Care bathrooms.

"He didn't do anything!" shouted Sheldon in a booming voice from his now-customary stage in the cafeteria. "Never before has someone who 'hasn't done anything' done so much!"

"He's too modest to talk about his achievements!" hollered Paul to a wildly agreeing crowd.

"We don't have to talk about his achievements!" Sheldon added. "We know them! All we have to do is continue our support and triple efforts!"

"Hooray!" cheered the LaPazes, who were good at triple efforts.

Peter Eversleigh did his bit by repeatedly offering Mike licorice.

"No thanks," Mike would say.

"Okay, dude. But should you experience the desire for this confection of which we are speaking, my stockpile of sticks is yours,"

While this new treatment was unusual, it was not

particularly uncomfortable, and Mike had no trouble pursuing his daily life. His admirers were enormously considerate of his desire to be alone, seeing him as a man with many burdens who needed time for contemplation. He was also regarded with a certain amount of awe, as many could not begin to imagine the thoughts of this quiet person who had accomplished so much.

"Give the dude his space," Peter Eversleigh advised. "A dude such as Mike needs to be given space in which to conceptualize."

Mike came to the conclusion that the only explanation for all this was that he was very, very famous. It was just another one of the things at this school that he didn't understand.

At first, Mr. Gamble decided to ignore the rumblings of discontent about the Mike Otis dismissal. After all, how long could they last? These *were* Don't Care students.

There was great interest among the staff, especially Mr. Morrison, to observe the students in a state in which they were never found before — motivated and united. In fact, the art and shop teachers did not even try to discourage the activities in support of Mike Otis, since the quality of that work showed more life and fire than ever before. The occasional rally in the cafeteria and hall was tolerated so long as general peace was maintained. The original staff consensus was to observe.

By the end of Mike's first week out of office, however, the litter problem was becoming critical. All walls and lockers were covered with posters and photographs, including some bizarre creations both inside and outside the school that impeded free movement. Not only was the school an eyesore, but there was even a staff casualty. Mr. Willis slipped on an eight-by-ten glossy and sprained his ankle. Mr. Gamble demanded action, but the staff and Mr. Morrison persuaded him to hold off.

The next week, Mr. Gamble knew right off the bat that he had made the wrong decision. The litter problem was raging out of control, and paper supplies were dwindling at an astounding rate. Wall space was virtually impossible to find, and signs and photos were beginning to overlap each other. On Wednesday after school, Mr. Gamble cleared the building of all students, and assembled the entire janitorial staff for what Sheldon would later call "the administration flexing its muscles."

Sheldon and Paul stood outside the school and, when the dense black smoke started pouring out of the chimney, they knew that the trash burners were working to capacity.

They met after dinner to plan strategy. At ten o'clock, they took a walk past the school, where the burners were still going. The massive Otis campaign was almost gone by this time, including no fewer than three hundred eight-by-ten glossies of the student body ex-president.

Paul was feeling like flexing a few muscles of his own. "With the support we've got at this point, we could have it all up again by the end of the week!"

Sheldon shook his head. "Tomorrow, Gamble's going to cut off the paper supply."

Paul stopped in his tracks. "How do you know?"

Sheldon shrugged. "*I* would have done it a week ago. He's also going to close the darkroom, art rooms, and all the shops as soon as class hours are out. And for good measure, I figure he's going to threaten to suspend anyone who tacks so much as a three-by five file card to a bulletin board."

"How do you know he's going to do it all at once?" asked Paul.

"The staff let all this go because they couldn't believe it would happen at Don't Care High. That's why they waited so long before cracking down. But now that it's stopping, it's stopping for good."

"Don't tell me we've lost, then?"

"Oh, no," said Sheldon. "That's the funny part. In fact, from here on in, we can't lose."

Paul was confused. "How do you figure that?"

They stopped walking and sat down on a small park bench.

"Just in case your campaign fever has made you forget," Sheldon explained, "Mike never ran for president, and after that, he never did a thing for the school. We made all that up, and the big danger was that everyone else would lose interest, and the two of us would be caught standing there holding up the flag. But now all twenty-six hundred kids love Mike — with or without us. They're all on a campaign that Mr. Gamble is shooting down. So now there's a conflict that we didn't have to manufacture. All the things that could land us in the toilet are way in the past. Now we're just two students in a whole united student body that has taken an interest in a school matter — the student body president."

"Will Mike ever be president again?"

"We'll keep working on it," Sheldon promised. "But now that the whole school is all for Mike, everything can be on the up-and-up. It's the plain campaign of a student body that had its president taken away for no reason. We're the good guys."

"So we're not just making trouble, then?"

"Of course not! At least, not anymore. Look at Wayne-o. He used to like Mike because he fixed the can. Now he just likes Mike, period. We had to use all that underhanded stuff to achieve a very important and unselfish goal. And now we've done it. Don't Care High *cares*."

Paul slapped his knee suddenly. "Sheldon, you may be a genius just like your mother!"

Sheldon laughed modestly. "Now that you trust my judgment so much, how are you for some Greek food? I know a place not far from here where the souvlaki melts in your mouth."

"And lies like a rock in your stomach," added Paul feelingly.

"Don't be a wet blanket. Zeus himself would come down off Mount Olympus to eat this stuff. Come on. Life is too short not to live a little."

9

May I have your attention, please. Just a few announcements from Mr. Gamble, which he says are important.

Even though the lighting in the halls is wanting, you have probably noticed that all posters, pictures, and other paraphernalia have been removed overnight. From here on, there will be no use of school paper and materials without approval and supervision by staff. School facilities such as the darkroom, art room, metal and print shops are off limits to students outside of class hours. Anyone caught posting a bill without staff approval will be suspended.

A roar of discontent went up throughout the school.

> *If this seems rather severe, may I reas-*
> *sure you that the staff will not take any*
> *hostages, and that public hangings will*
> *be discouraged. That's all. Have a*
> *good day.*

The students were bitter. After homeroom, they met in large and small groups and exchanged gripes and opinions. Plaintive voices rang in the halls. Some of the groups approached Sheldon and Paul with thoughts of revolution.

"Calm down," said Sheldon soothingly. "We're on the side of what's right and good. We can't lose. But let's not do anything stupid. Mike doesn't want that."

Despite Sheldon's calm confidence, Paul was not satisfied with the new situation. Mike was still out of office, and the idea of doing nothing rankled. He went through the day constantly expecting Sheldon to announce a massive plan of attack to reinstate Mike, but Sheldon seemed quite happy to let the matter simmer.

After school, Paul was forced to turn his mind to other problems, for today he was scheduled for his first New York haircut. His appointment had been made by Auntie Nancy personally, so the warning bells were ringing loud and clear in Paul's head as he walked into Edmondo's Creations.

Auntie Nancy had arranged for Paul to have Edmondo himself. How can she stand to be so good to me? he thought, as Edmondo ran his fingers through Paul's hair experimentally, sizing up the *ambience* of the cut that was forthcoming.

"Just a normal trim, please," said Paul nervously.

"Ah, normal. What is normal? If you will just allow me to study your face for a moment, I shall assess the balance and composition. There is only one correct affectation to every *visage*, only one style that truly is, as you say, normal."

Paul shut his mouth and eyes, determined to endure, while Edmondo went to work on him, clipping artfully and humming arias from *The Barber of Seville*. When it was all over, Paul allowed himself to look at the man he had become. He stifled a cry of shock. His neat wavy brown locks had become a halo of tight, riotous ringlets that framed his face like a bonnet.

Paul paid his staggering bill, left a large tip because Auntie Nancy had told him to, and escaped to the street. There he found his reflection in a store window and tried to smooth down his curls with frantic hands. Nothing helped. Edmondo was a top-notch barber. He had cut so well that the only way to deprogram this hair would be to attend to each curl individually. He finally had to settle for a bit of a flat-top with stick-out bangs — all rather messy, but at least it looked sort of like Paul Abrams. Confidence somewhat restored, he started out for the subway and home.

He was planning sarcastic comments to fire at his mother when he heard a cry of pain, and Edmondo appeared out of nowhere, scooped him up off the sidewalk, and hustled him back inside into the chair, displacing another customer with,

"I'm sorry, sir! You'll have to wait! This is an emergency!" He turned to Paul, his voice thick with agitation. *"What happened to your hair?"*

"It was . . . uh . . . windy," explained Paul, despising himself.

"No, no, no!" cried Edmondo as he set about restoring his desecrated creation to its former glory. This time he sprayed each ringlet with a generous shot of hair spray before sending Paul on his way. "Be careful!"

Paul knew care wasn't necessary. You couldn't have moved this hairdo with a bulldozer.

As he headed for the subway, he realized that he was walking past the parking garage into which Mike Otis had disappeared the day he and Sheldon had followed him. It was a bit of a jolt to his system, as the mad pace of recent events had caused him to put the mystery of Mike out of mind. He quickened his step and then stopped short. There was a sign on the entrance which he and Sheldon had missed the first time around, probably because of the layers of dirt that covered it. It read:

RESIDENTIAL PARKING: ENTER HERE AND DRIVE THROUGH INNER GATE.

His heart began to pound. An inner gate! That had to explain Mike's disappearance! Forgetting his haircut, he rushed right over to Sheldon's house.

Sheldon opened the door, took one look at him, and collapsed into laughter.

118

Mrs. Pryor, the genius, appeared in the hallway. "Shelly, is that any way to treat a friend? You must be Paul. Hello, I'm Sheldon's mother."

"He looks like Little Orphan Annie!" Sheldon gasped, holding onto a wall for support.

Paul felt himself turning mauve.

"Don't pay any attention to him," interrupted his sister, Jodi. "I think it looks fine."

Paul was also introduced to Sheldon's little brother, Harvey, who thought hair was unimportant, and Sheldon's father, who sat at the dining room table examining colored boarding passes with tweezers and magnifying glass.

"This is Sheldon's friend, Paul," said Jodi.

"Hi, Paul. Flown anywhere lately?"

"Let's go upstairs," said Sheldon finally. "Flash Flood's doing one of his big retrospectives today. We can't miss it."

Once in Sheldon's room, Paul excitedly told of his findings. "This has got to be it, Shel. We staked out the only two doors to the garage, but this inner gate must lead to another parking area with other doors and probably elevators right into the neighboring apartment buildings. Mike must live in one of those buildings."

Sheldon grinned broadly. "Neat bit of detective work, Ambition. But tomorrow the real investigation starts. We're going to find out about Mike's secret life. Are you up to it?"

"Of course I'm up to it," said Paul. Which was exactly what Steve would have said.

The next day right after school, Sheldon and Paul

staked out the parking garage, hiding behind a small Buick just inside the main entrance. By this time, Paul's bravado had mellowed.

"You know, Shel, if this is all on the up-and-up, why are we hiding? People who are on the up-and-up shouldn't have to hide."

"Take my word for it, Ambition, this is the best approach. We have here a guy who gives a phony address and telephone number to the school. I don't like it any more than you do, but finding him out calls for a little espionage."

"Don't give me that, Sheldon. You love this. You're having the time of your life."

Sheldon favored him with a crooked grin. "It shows, does it?"

At that moment, the light from the street was blotted out as a large vehicle entered the garage.

"This is it!" exclaimed Sheldon.

The two watched as the black behemoth whispered by their position and headed deeper into the garage. They followed, keeping low and in the shadows as Mike drove up to a metal barrier, inserted his key in a switch on the wall, and waited as the gate began to lift. He drove through, and the grill started to descend. Sheldon and Paul made a mad dash, diving under the gate just in time. They hid behind a post, catching their breath, as Mike parked his car and headed for a bank of elevators. When the elevator had borne Mike away, they rushed over and checked the indicator.

"He got off at seven," Sheldon breathed triumphantly. "Now we check out the lobby."

The mailboxes were in a remote corner of the main floor. They examined the 7's and, sure enough, box 7E bore the single word *Otis*.

"Now what?" asked Paul. "Surely we're not going to ride up there and knock on his door."

"Close," said Sheldon. "We're going to get on the fire escape and look in his window."

Paul was aghast. "That's the stupidest idea I've ever heard!"

"Well, do you want to buzz him? I'll let you explain what we're here for."

"Aw, Shel!"

"Have I mentioned my fear of heights?" said Paul as the two climbed from the roof onto the fire escape. "And how about my mother's lectures? I've already got one coming for the grime I picked up in the garage. I'll bet there's an even better one for dashing my brains out on the sidewalk."

Sheldon ignored him. "The E apartments are on this corner. We're in perfect position."

They climbed down to the seventh floor and looked into the first window. The room was a frilly pink affair with a canopy bed and posters of bubble-gum pop stars on the walls. On the back of the door hung a cheerleader's outfit and two purple and white pompoms.

"Strange," Sheldon mused.

They checked the next window. This was definitely a boy's room, but the decor of the place clearly indicated that it could not possibly have anything to do with Mike. The walls were plastered with posters of sports heroes and pennants from various universities. Countless model airplanes hung from the ceiling, with another under construction on the floor.

"Well, obviously there's been some mistake," Sheldon murmured.

The third window looked into the kitchen, where the mother of the family was cooking dinner while chatting with her son and daughter, ages about eleven and fourteen. The window was open, and Sheldon and Paul could hear that the conversation centered on school cheerleading practice and the latest Ranger game.

"I don't know where we blew it," whispered Sheldon, "but this is definitely the wrong apartment."

Paul was looking in the last window. "No, it's not. Shel, get over here."

The two crouched by the sill and peered inside. This room was smaller than the others and completely bare except for a small bed, bureau, and desk. The white walls were totally unadorned and, except for the bed linens, there was really only one indication that the place was inhabited — on the desk chair was draped a large beige raincoat.

Sheldon's face radiated deep adoration. "It's Mike," he said ecstatically. "And he's taken off his raincoat. He really lets his hair down at home."

Back at the kitchen, Mike had joined his mother, brother, and sister. There he sat, sipping at a tall glass of water while the conversation continued, enveloping but not including him.

Paul was almost relieved to see that Mike was

pretty much the same at home as he was at school, answering only direct questions.

"How about that Ranger game, Mike?"

"I didn't see it."

"Can you make it to my cheerleading practice tonight, Mike?"

"No."

This was the night the Otis family ate early, as Dad had bowling, Mom had bridge club, Susie had cheerleading practice, and Chuck had a Boy Scout meeting. Mike did not seem to have any plans.

Sheldon and Paul crouched at the kitchen window, peeking in and listening to the conversation. Sheldon seemed delighted with each boring detail, but Paul just grew more confused and frustrated. How could this scene out of *Leave It to Beaver* be Mike's family? How could these ordinary, wholesome people not notice that Mike looked nothing like them, acted nothing like them, dressed nothing like them, thought nothing like them, and spoke not at all at their dinner table? And strangest of all, what was Paul Abrams doing perching on a fire escape, spying on a family eating dinner, seven stories and two thousand miles away from Saskatoon?

"Pssst! Shel! Let's get out of here!"

Sheldon did not seem to hear him. They held their position as the conversation went from dull to uninteresting to mundane and back again. Finally, Mr. Otis decided it was time for some family business.

"Michael, I phoned your school today to talk to

your teachers and check on your progress. According to your physics teacher, you're getting a failing grade in her class."

Mike did not respond. His expression was essentially the same one he had held all year and, presumably, since the day of his birth.

Mr. Otis was undaunted. "Mrs. Nelson says the only way you can pass is by doing a major display project."

Another silence.

"Are you going to do the project?"

"I haven't thought about it," said Mike.

Mr. Otis then launched into an elaborate lecture about "taking your education seriously" which was worthy of Paul's mother. Mike just sat at the table and let it all bounce off him. Paul was so wrapped up in the drama unfolding in the Otis residence that he didn't notice the look of determination coming over Sheldon's face.

"We've seen enough, Ambition. Let's split."

As they left the building, this time through the lobby, Paul's head was spinning. "Things made more sense when he lived on the eleventh floor of a ten-story building. At least then there was a possible explanation — he's the leader of an international spy ring, he's from another planet, that sort of thing. I could have bought that. But him coming from this . . . this lovely family. . . ."

Sheldon's mind was elsewhere. "Mike's failing physics. Do you know what that means? It means the staff will have a good reason to keep him out of office. We can't allow him to fail."

"Hold it, Shel. It's not exactly up to us. If Mike

does his extra project, he'll pass. If he doesn't — "

Paul caught the look on his friend's face. "You're not suggesting that we do the project for him!"

"Not exactly," said Sheldon. "But think of all the kids at school. They're frustrated. They're complaining that they should be doing something to help Mike. *Here's* something they can do to help Mike. I'll bet if we put out a call for volunteers, they'd come flocking by the hundreds."

"To do Mike's work for him?"

"To *help* Mike catch up on work he missed because he was so busy with his presidential duties. When you think of all his accomplishments, it's no wonder he fell behind in one of his classes. And the last couple of weeks must have been really trying for him."

"Remember who you're talking about," Paul reminded him. "You're not going to have an easy time explaining all this to Mike."

"Mike'll be grateful to have help with his project," Sheldon insisted. "And we'll even con him into coming forward to bless it or something, so the volunteers will know we're on the level."

"What if Mrs. Nelson finds out Mike didn't do the project?" challenged Paul.

"Impossible," Sheldon replied airily. "And after all Mike's done for the students of this school, I'm surprised that you even have to think about this. You should be jumping at the chance to give the guy a hand."

As they walked down the subway steps, Paul played his last trump card. "If you're going to have a project, you're going to need a topic."

Sheldon smiled engagingly. "There *is* only one topic for the true leader of Don't Care High — the sewer."

Mike's educational problems met with great sympathy from the Don't Care student body. Samuel Wiscombe summarized everyone's attitude: "I'm not much for science projects, but if this is what Mike needs me to do, then I'm all for it."

Sheldon put out the call for volunteers during the three lunch periods from his usual post atop the dining hall end table.

"Mike put so much of his heart and soul into representing you that he even let his education slip! Now that he's out of office, our true leader has more on his mind than ever before. That's why he needs your help. I want volunteers every day at three-thirty in the physics lab to give Mike a hand with his project. Remember, every minute you give to him is one more that he can devote to getting back into office for the good of us all!"

And it worked. Paul could hardly believe his eyes when, at three-thirty, several hundred selfless volunteers packed the lab area, the work area, and even the adjacent office, champing at the bit for the chance to help with Mike's project. No one seemed to notice that the project he was "helping" with presently stood at point zero and consisted only of a small sign reading THE SEWER SYSTEM, BY MIKE OTIS. Nor did anyone mind that Mike himself was not present, since Sheldon explained that the true leader was off contemplating the dilemma of his return to power. In lieu of Mike, Sheldon had hung an eight-by-ten glossy of the chief executive over the work area for inspiration.

As Paul watched in a state of combined admiration and horror, Sheldon shamelessly deployed his troops. The more mechanically inclined were sent to build the various miniature models of pipes, pumps, and reservoirs. Others were sent with them to explain these models, and still others were loosed upon the city's many libraries to research the topic from both a scientific and an historical standpoint. A group of ten were sent to research the specific contributions of Don Carey himself, but that still left about twenty people whose talents were as yet unemployed.

So Sheldon explained to the leftovers that they were an elite group, handpicked for their creative thinking ability. "You guys are going to do a section about what's in the future for the sewer system. Mike calls it 'Whither Sewage.' " He addressed the whole group again. "Okay. Now, we'll meet here every day at three-thirty for progress reports. Remember — you're working for Mike now, and that's a very important privilege. Okay, let's go!"

When everyone had gone off, Paul turned on his friend. "Well, I suppose you're proud of yourself!"

"Why?"

"You know perfectly well why! You just lined everybody up for tons of work when you yourself are doing absolutely nothing!"

"That's not true," said Sheldon righteously. "You and I are operating in a supervisory capacity. We're coordinating all the individual efforts."

"Yeah, but the fact remains that everyone else is

off doing research and stuff, and we're lying around."

"Didn't I mention it? We have the hardest job of all. It's our responsibility to start right now convincing Mike that this really is his project, and that he has to act like he did it. So, as you can see, Ambition, we're not shirking in any way."

"Okay," said Paul, "but how about that snow job you just gave everybody, about how they're helping Mike instead of catering to your whims? How about those creative souls handpicked to explore the sewers of tomorrow? 'Whither Sewage'! How's poor Mike going to explain *that* to Mrs. Nelson?"

Sheldon shrugged. "We'll get Mike to downplay it a little. You worry too much, Ambition. It's going to be great."

Explaining it to Mike was tough. Immediately after the recruitment meeting, Sheldon and Paul found the ex-president and related the whole idea of "The Sewer System." Paul was afraid that Mike would ask how they knew he needed a project to up his physics grade. In fact, he needn't have worried, as Mike's confusion was far more general.

"This is my project." It was not a question, but not quite a statement of fact either. Mike's monotone was suffused with perplexity.

"Right," said Sheldon.

"But I'm not doing a project."

"Exactly. You don't have to, because we're helping you out with this one."

"I get a project and I don't have to do anything?"

"Right."

"How?"

Sheldon wasn't sure exactly what that question was asking, so he gave Mike his prepared answer for "Why?" He explained how Mike had done so much as student body president, and how everyone was anxious to pay him back through "The Sewer System."

Mike paused for a long time. Finally, he said, "This seems strange." After tending to his left safety pin, which was slipping, he shut his locker, gave Sheldon and Paul a haunted bye and headed for the stairwell.

"Now what are we going to do?" moaned Paul. "You've got hundreds of people slaving their butts off, and Mike won't even go along with it. How are we going to call them all back?"

"Call them back?" Sheldon was unperturbed. "Mike just needs a little time to mull things over and get used to the idea. In the end, he'll be grateful. Even he can't turn down a free project."

Then a crisis arose. Feldstein imposed a school-wide, comprehensive locker ban on the project. Sheldon and Paul first got wind of it when Phil Gonzalez reported that the locker baron had turned down his request for locker space in which to store his model materials.

"It's the old locker grudge," said Sheldon. "Feldstein's still sore over his 200C series. This could be a drag."

Some students tried to avoid the ban by denying any connection to "The Sewer System." This was successful at first, but Feldstein quickly caught on and became vigilant, exacting harsh penalties on violators. Dan Wilburforce was caught using a Feldstein locker to store library books on the life of Don Carey. He lost the locker, and it cost him a turkey cutlet to keep his second one in the English wing. He didn't dare store his Don Carey books there, though, as he was on permanent locker probation. Cindy Schwartz, a repeat violator, had all four of her lockers taken away. Feldstein was even severe with the minor violators, handing out fines of twenty- and even twenty-four-inch pizzas for using Feldstein lockers on the project.

Sheldon was nervous. "There's more to it than just the 200C grudge," he told Paul. "I've been checking around, and ever since Mike's rise to power, the locker business has been going down the drain."

Paul was mystified. "What's Mike got to do with the locker business?"

"You take twenty-six hundred kids who can't get up any interest in school or extracurricular stuff, and put them in this building six and a half hours a day. What do you think about? Having well-located lockers, having a lot of lockers, having lockers placed all over the school so they never have to walk very far with books to get to their classes. Lockers are the economy of this place."

"But what's so different about now?" Paul asked.

"Now they're all dedicating their lives to Mike. They've got an interest, so the locker business dies. During the whole poster campaign, Feldstein didn't make a single deal. No wonder he's angry."

"Shel, you're forgetting how *weird* all this is. I come from Saskatoon, where if you tell somebody

130

that there's a locker ban, he doesn't know what you're talking about. Think about this for a minute. We're commandeering hundreds of lives, getting them to work on a project all about sewers on behalf of a guy who nobody understands, and who doesn't even want our help, and we're doing all this in a police state while trying to steer clear of the one-man locker Gestapo. Now does that make sense?"

Sheldon was abstracted. "We have got to see Feldstein."

Feldstein's resolve was unshakable. "I want you to know that I've got nothing against you, man. But this is business, and business is something different. If my business is on the ropes, I do what I have to do to fix it. If someone wants to take that personally — well, that's too bad. But that's me, man."

Despite himself, Paul felt a faint twinge of admiration for the locker baron. He could see that Sheldon, too, was affected by Feldstein's speech. They left the stairwell with no hard feelings, each shaking the locker baron's hand and wishing him all the best.

Once out in the hall, Paul turned to his friend. "Well, now what?"

"We've got a real problem," Sheldon agreed. "Except for Mike, Feldstein's the most influential guy in school. Already the progress reports on 'The Sewer System' are slowing down. This locker ban is making people stop and think, and our workers are losing their sense of direction."

"What can we do?"

"There's only one thing we *can* do," said Sheldon, the characteristic grin returning to his face. "Congregate and inspire."

The next day, Sheldon called together all the workers in the physics lab. "Mike knows about our problems, and he's sorry he can't be here today. But he sent me to read a message from him to you."

Paul watched in shock as Sheldon unfolded a sheet of blank paper and, pretending to read from it, launched into an inspirational speech worthy of Moses. The workers, crammed belly to belly in the lab and surrounding areas, gave Sheldon their absolute and undivided attention as he spoke the words of the student body ex-president. Paul knew a brief moment of fear as he saw Mike himself pass the lab door, hear his name mentioned, and glance inside. He left quickly, though, having no trouble recognizing the goings-on as an offshoot of one of the things at this school that he didn't understand.

Sheldon finished with, "'I realize how hard it is to work on a major science project without locker space, and that's why I don't blame any of you if you want to give this up. I just want you all to know that, one way or the other, it was an honor serving as your student body president, an office which I hope to hold again in the near future.' "

The lab rang with applause.

Not one of the workers gave up on "The Sewer System." Even the lockerless Cindy Schwartz, now forced to wander the halls with all her worldly possessions in a Bloomingdale's bag, was not discour-

132

aged. Rallying to the call of Mike's impassioned message, the students dug in and fairly exploded with effort.

Daily at three-thirty, Sheldon, Paul, and the eight-by-ten glossy were presented with glowing progress reports by all groups as the project began to take shape. Networks of miniature sewer pipes sprouted from nowhere as the model committees worked around the clock. Graphs, maps, and diagrams were appearing en masse. Each day, the research teams submitted piles of material to be collated and reorganized by other researchers, who were in turn submitting material to the first teams. All work eventually found its way to the typing desks of the LaPaz triplets, who claimed to do the job three times as efficiently as anyone else. No one questioned this.

The operations were widespread. It was impossible to walk any distance in Don Carey High School without running into several facets of the project, as the work had long since moved out of the confines of the physics lab. Since lockers were forbidden, materials were stored almost anywhere. Based on what was called "The Wayne-o Loophole," after its originator, supplies would be taken from school storerooms and placed in individual lockers so that project materials could be stored in their place without violating Feldstein's ban.

Though only a small percentage of the student body was actively working on the project, many others volunteered to run errands and be generally helpful, and virtually all of the school was interested in supporting Mike's big effort.

Mike himself was aware that a new breed of question had begun to invade his cocoon. Students were coming up to him and saying, "How's the sewer project coming along, Mike?" Or "Were you able to make any use of that diagram I drew up last night?" Many times, a smile and a nod were not enough for these people, and it was necessary for him to speak. He assumed that the project was the same one mentioned in his most recent conversation with those two guys, the ones who kept coming to him with unusual things to say. He did not know what the connection was, nor did he want to know, as it was obviously another one of the things at this school he didn't understand.

Mike's participation, beyond his photograph, was not necessary, however, as Sheldon was definitely in charge. At three-thirty, he took possession of the physics office and settled himself in the swivel chair, crossing his legs and resting his feet on the desk top. He called himself the project's nerve center, but he had delegated the responsibility so well that it left him nothing to do. Every now and then, he would randomly select a few pieces of paper to approve, like Dick Oliver's city sewer map, or Cindy Schwartz's pictorial representation of the life and times of Don Carey. The rest of the time he spent in conversation with members of his elite group of intellectual commandos, which Paul had taken to calling the Stink-Tank Think-Tank.

Paul felt that *he* was the true nerve center of the operation, because he was having a near-nervous breakdown imagining what would happen to himself and Sheldon if Mike denied any connection to the project. If the Mike Otis hoax ever became known to the president's twenty-six hundred devotees, Paul's life and Sheldon's wouldn't be worth an oompah out of Slim Kroy's big brass tuba.

By the next Friday, even Paul had to admit that the project was a good one. Though it was based on a joke topic, there really did seem to be a lot to be said about the sewer system, and the information of the project was pertinent and well-presented. There were visual aids, such as graphs, charts, diagrams, and maps; and the working models were particularly impressive.

After class, all of the materials were organized and set up in the large, attractive display case built by Samuel Wiscombe, Dick Oliver, and Dan Wilburforce. The three had become very close friends in Mike's service, and claimed to be a trio rivaling even the LaPaz triplets. They called themselves the "WOW Connection." It didn't bother them a bit that the name never caught on.

When the project was all assembled, it was an impressive sight. The words THE SEWER SYSTEM, BY MIKE OTIS gleamed in silver sparkles, flanked by an eight-by-ten glossy on either side. The working models sat on the bottom, and the information was arranged in booklets strategically placed around the display. The attractive city sewer map was placed front and center, with heavy flow pipes drawn in bright red, and light flow pipes in a more conservative blue. Directly to the right of that was the section on the life and career of Don Carey, which was well done, if a little dry. It was certainly not the fault of the students that Don Carey had been a boring person.

The only reservations Paul held about the project were in the "Whither Sewage" section. This was the product of Sheldon's elite group of storm drain visionaries, the Stink-Tank Think-Tank. The group, which included such members as Peter Eversleigh, Trudy Helfield, and Wayne-o, had come up with a fifteen-page booklet outlining in great detail four original proposals for the disposal of sewage waste:

1) Package sewage in sealed containers and drop it in the deepest part of the world's oceans.

2) Incinerate sewage using the heat of the earth's core by dropping it into dormant volcanoes.

3) Develop heavy-duty, low-cost rockets for the purpose of firing sewage into outer space.

4) Construct a pipeline to convey all sewage to Greenland.

But setting aside "Whither Sewage," the effort was excellent, and everyone was agreed that Mike Otis was a brilliant student as well as a wonderful president.

Paul allowed himself a laugh as Sheldon called for a round of applause for Mike, but his laugh came out a nervous giggle. He had a deep, gut feeling that something would go wrong with "The Sewer System."

Meanwhile, Mr. Morrison was undergoing the great crisis of his career. Ever since his arrival at Don Carey, he had been trying desperately to motivate the students. What did he get in return? An indifferent student body, and co-workers who laughed at him. He could still hear Mr. Gamble's voice more than eight years ago — his first day at Don Carey — saying, "These kids can be difficult. Don't beat your head against the wall." And then, just a few short weeks later, "You're beating your head against the wall."

It was true. He could still feel those twinges of pain as all his valiant attempts to stimulate the students fizzled into nothing, one by one: the Yearbook Society, the Social Committee, Students for Don Carey, the Welcoming Committee. Even the General Interest Group had attracted no interest. He could hear the principal's deep, mocking baritone announcing that yet another one of his projects had bitten the dust "due to lack of interest." How many nights had he lain awake in his bed hatching brilliant schemes, only to have them fall victim to that relentless monster called "lack of interest?" He'd given so much of himself to Don Carey High, and what was his reward? Ridicule from the teachers, blank stares from students, a small fortune in analyst's bills, and a carload of unsold raffle tickets.

Now everything was different. The students were motivated and active. They finally had a purpose. And it was his job to tell them that they were wrong. The irony of it was driving him crazy. How many years had he prayed for the day when student activities would become more than an abstract concept? And yet, when that great day arrived, Arthur Morrison was on the other team.

Each morning his student suggestion box was

full of politely-worded requests for the reinstatement of the student body president. He had yet to see one slip of paper that dealt with any other topic. Each day, his appointment book was full, and at fifteen-minute intervals, he interviewed students who had come to guidance to express their frustration over the handling of the Otis affair. None would accept the clear and untarnished truth that Mike Otis had had nothing to do with his own candidacy.

Twenty-six hundred informed, motivated kids, taking an interest in student government through civilized and peaceful means — any guidance counselor's dream. It was within his grasp; so close, yet so far. So what if Mike never ran for president? He didn't *mind* being president. If Gamble would just let him back into office, the possibilities with these students would be limitless! But no. Gamble would be stubborn, and the opportunity would be lost. And once again, Arthur Morrison would walk the barren wasteland stalked by that inevitable monster called "lack of interest."

10

Monday morning before classes, Sheldon and Paul presented "The Sewer System" to Mike. It took the two of them to carry the large display case through the hall and set it in front of Mike's locker. Then they waited, Sheldon in undisguised pride, Paul in extreme anxiety.

A few minutes later, Mike's face appeared in the window of the heavy stairwell doors. He came no closer, though, but instead stared through the glass at the project in bland perplexity. Then he turned around and disappeared from view.

It took a few seconds for Sheldon and Paul to realize what was happening. They caught up with Mike in the parking lot, hunching towards the black behemoth.

"Hey, Mike," said Sheldon, "where are you going?"

Mike didn't stop. "Home."

"But it's only eight forty-five. Classes haven't even started yet." No response. "Why are you leaving now?"

Finally, Mike stopped. He looked squarely at Sheldon and Paul. "I don't think this is going to be a good day."

"But you can't leave!" blurted Paul. "Your project is ready to be handed in today."

During the silence that followed, Paul stared into Mike's distant eyes. For one brief moment, he wondered if the flood of questions he thought he saw there might suddenly pour out and inundate them. Instead, there was just one word.

"No."

Sheldon decided to be firm. "What do you mean, *no*? After everybody's hard work — *no*? If you don't hand in this project, you'll fail physics!"

Mike paused again. "Do I have to do anything?"

"No! Nothing at all!" Paul said quickly. "We'll even carry it for you. All you have to say is 'Here's my project, Mrs. Nelson.' "

"Here's my project, Mrs. Nelson," repeated Mike.

"Perfect," approved Sheldon. "Let's go."

They found Mrs. Nelson in the physics office. Mike spoke his line, and Sheldon and Paul placed the project beside her desk. At this point, Mike tried to leave, assuming that since his part was over, maybe he was no longer needed. But Paul put an iron grip on his shoulder.

Mrs. Nelson was amazed. First she walked back and forth in front of the project as though trying to look at it from all angles. Then she began leafing through the information booklets, illustrations, and diagrams. Sheldon operated the working models for her, trying his best to appear as though Mike were directing him.

"Does it hook up this way, Mike?"

"Sure."

As Mrs. Nelson went through the whole project, a wide smile took root and spread across her normally severe face. She looked a little confused at "Whither Sewage," but much to Paul's great relief, she let it pass.

"Congratulations, Michael. This is the most wonderful project I've seen in all my years of teaching!" The teacher raved up and down about the effort, and spoke of how pleased and surprised she was. Sheldon beamed with pride, and even Paul felt a great deal of satisfaction over the project's reception. Mrs. Nelson obviously didn't suspect any irregularities, and through it all, Mike looked marginally aware of what was happening. Everything was going along beautifully until Mrs. Nelson announced her intention of entering "The Sewer System" in the Citywide High School Science Fair, which was taking place at the Midtown Community Center on Wednesday.

Paul turned deathly pale, but Sheldon smiled even wider. "That's great news, isn't it, Mike?"

"Very good."

When they had left the physics office and Mike had made his escape, Paul turned on his friend. "You're sick, you know that? How could you agree to participate in that science fair? Oh, I can't believe you did it! Why couldn't you make up some dumb excuse like Mike has a doctor's appointment, or a dentist appointment, or a safety pin polishing appointment?"

"Cool it, Ambition. This is a great opportunity. If Mike can win this science fair, think of what it'll mean!"

"Shel, we barely got him to say 'Here's my project.' How can you possibly expect him to compete in a science fair?"

"He was right there with us when Mrs. Nelson brought it up," Sheldon argued, "and he didn't protest."

"That's because he had no idea what was going on, and he didn't want to know," Paul retorted. "If I hadn't been holding him, he would've made a bolt for the door. This is crazy."

"Look, you're the one who's always complaining about Don't Care High. Well, here you go! Now we have our first science fair entry in . . . in . . . I don't think anybody knows how many years."

May I have your attention, please. Just one announcement. On Wednesday, the Citywide High School Science Fair competition will take place at the Midtown Community Center. On that day, we were to have achieved the distinction of being the first school ever to go without an entry for forty years. However, I have just been informed that, due to a sudden outburst of interest, Mike Otis will be representing Don Carey High School this year.

There was cheering in all homerooms. The teachers were stunned at the fact that Mike Otis, who ought to have been a dead issue at this point, was resurfacing.

When Sheldon and Paul went after Mike to remind him to attend the science fair, Mike seemed to have a game plan of his own. He stood his ground in the conversation, and whenever something he didn't understand came up, he simply said, "No."

"But everyone's counting on you!" protested Sheldon.

"On me," Mike repeated.

"Exactly. So you have to go to the science fair with us on Wednesday afternoon. That's all."

Mike thought about it for a long time. Then he said, "No."

"Oh, please!" Paul blurted. "We *need* you to be there! You have no idea how much we need you to be there!"

Mike looked haunted. "I won't have to do anything there?"

"Not a thing," said Sheldon quickly. "Nothing at all. We'll do everything."

"Well, then, I guess I can go." There was a pause as Sheldon and Paul looked at him, awaiting more.

"I should eat lunch now," said Mike, looking extremely uncomfortable.

"Sure!" said Sheldon. "No problem. We'll get right out of your way. Thanks a lot, Mike."

On Wednesday morning, the principal urged all students to drop by the science fair after classes when the prizes were to be awarded. Sheldon did him one better, however, spreading the word that Mike expected a good turnout for the judging, which was to begin at one-thirty.

"The fair is open to the public," Sheldon reasoned, "so we'll get a gang in there to ooh and aah over Mike's project when the judges are looking. It can't hurt to stack the audience a little."

As the head of the science department, Mr. Schmidt was obligated to drive Sheldon, Paul, and the project to the Midtown Community Center. Clearly, though, he did not wish to be associated with "The Sewer System," and once inside the building, made himself extremely scarce. He avoided all his colleagues — apparently afraid that they were going to laugh at him — promised to be back for the presentations, and disappeared.

Mike wasn't due to arrive until one, but Sheldon and Paul had everything set up by eleven-thirty. There was light traffic among the booths, mostly adults, and Don Carey High School's first entry in forty years was the center of much attention. The boys took some kidding, and smiled bravely through a lot of sewer jokes. The fair officials were shocked by the project. Anything at all from Don Carey High was completely unexpected; the end result of so much work was astonishing.

Paul let Sheldon field the questions about Mike, which Sheldon did casually by saying, "Oh, Mike'll be here soon. He's just tied up somewhere — busy man, you know."

Many of the spectators had heard about Mike's brief sojourn as student body president, and expressed an interest in meeting him.

"That's really impressive," commented one teacher. "It's quite an accomplishment to get that kind of enthusiasm from Don't Care — uh — your school."

"I hope you get a chance to meet Mike," said Sheldon glibly. "He's not what you'd expect. He's very quiet."

At noon, Mr. Morrison arrived, his face flushed with excitement as he attended his first ever extra-curricular activity as a Don Carey staff member. He stood proudly in front of the booth, hailing all the people he knew and making sure all were aware that Don Carey had an entry this year. In his opinion, this science fair was the first step on the school's road back to respectability, and he was aching to see the entry win a prize.

In another half hour, Paul began to notice some of the Don't Care students among the browsers. These were the usual prominent citizens in the Mike Otis scheme of things: Wayne-o, the LaPazes, and the WOW Connection. These people stayed away from the booth, though, to avoid being seen by Mr. Morrison, who might have wanted to know why they were not in class. He did see them eventually, but was so overwhelmed by the school spirit that had brought them there that he greeted them happily.

One o'clock came and went, and there were about twenty Don't Care students in circulation, but no Mike.

"I knew it!" Paul moaned. "I knew he wouldn't show up!"

"Shh, Ambition. He'll be here. Don't worry. He probably just got lost. Why don't you go to the door and look for him?"

Paul made his way to the hall's main entrance and poked his head outside. He gaped. The stairs, the sidewalk, and the lawns were teeming with Don't Care students — it looked like the whole school was there. A group of bewildered center security personnel had set up a rope barrier and were going through the motions of crowd control. But the students were peaceful. They swarmed behind the barrier and waited patiently for developments. At the head of the group was the massive Slim Kroy. He held his tuba high, like a standard, and all rallied behind it.

Rigid with shock, Paul hurried back to Sheldon and related the situation.

Sheldon broke into a broad grin. "What a great school we go to!"

"Shel, I don't think you realize the seriousness of the situation! It's one twenty-five, Mike's not here, and there are thousands of people out there who are going to blame us for the whole thing!"

Suddenly, a great cheer went up outside the building, and there was a rush to the front door as

146

the stirring strains of Slim Kroy's *Mike Otis Tuba Solo* wafted into the hall. And then he stood in the doorway, silhouetted by the bright afternoon sun — the student body ex-president and true leader of Don't Care High.

A murmur went up in the main hall as Sheldon and Paul both hurried over and hustled Mike to the project. Paul was too relieved to speak, but Sheldon babbled ecstatically about "The Sewer System" being the best effort in the place and no one else having a chance.

"Isn't it a beauty?" said Sheldon proudly.

Wayne-o sidled over to Mike. "The way I see it, you can't lose. There are only three other really classy-looking projects here. One's about solar energy, which is a big yawn; there's another called 'The Abiotic Synthesis of Organic Compounds,' which is a burn-out because who can understand that kind of stuff?; and the third is called 'You Can Live Beneath the Sea,' which is about settlements on the ocean floor. It's okay, but who's going to want to live beneath the sea with all that sewage dumped there? You're a cinch." To Paul he added, "Look how cool he is! Not a nervous bone in his body! A normal man would be sweating his guts out in this spot."

"I see what you mean," Paul agreed weakly.

The head judge approached. "Ah. The Sewer System. Quite a popular little entry you've got here." He checked the photographs and smiled at Mike. "Okay, first of all, do you certify that this is your own original work?"

"No."

A gasp went up in the immediate vicinity, and

Paul knew that it was all over. After that one little syllable, nothing anyone could say or do would save the hundreds of man-hours of work. The plug was pulled on "The Sewer System."

"What he means to say," Sheldon put in quickly, "is that we're . . . uh . . . a very cooperative school at Don't Care — Don Carey, so any one student's work is the work of the whole school, and — "

The judge ignored him and addressed Mike once again. "You had help?" There was no answer, so he asked, "What percentage of this project is your own work?"

Mike reverted to his stock answer. "I didn't do anything."

"Modest!" croaked Sheldon. "He's being modest! What a guy!"

"Do you understand the consequences of what you're saying, Mike?" the judge asked.

"Probably not," said Mike blandly.

The judge shook his head. "Well, I'm afraid I'm forced to disqualify this entry."

"Wait a minute here!" Mr. Morrison stormed onto the scene. "You can't disqualify this fine project just because of a . . . technicality!"

"I think this is more than a technicality," said the judge haughtily.

"But this is our first entry in forty years!"

The judge looked at him unkindly. "Well, then, someone at Don't Care High had plenty of time to see to it that it was done correctly!"

"It's not Don't Care High!" In a rage, the guidance counselor grabbed the brimming bucket of blue-dyed water that was to be used in the working model and sloshed it into the judge's face.

The judge then sacrificed what was left of his dignity and took a swing at Mr. Morrison, who ducked, and the man's fist made contact with a cage of twenty-five white mice. The cage sailed through the air and split in two as it hit the floor, its occupants scrambling in all directions.

Wayne-o sprinted to the door. "Mike's been disqualified!" he shouted to the waiting crowd. "After all his hard work, he's been disqualified!"

Slim Kroy was the first to react. "We've got to see him right away!" He leaped over the barrier and thundered into the hall. The rest of the students poured in after him, their one concern to reach the ex-president and console him in this moment of injustice.

May I have your attention, please. Here are the day's announcements.

Based on the number of classes that suffered from absenteeism yesterday, plus some eyewitness accounts, I conclude that many of you were present to watch our school participate in the City-wide High School Science Fair, which was postponed — a term I use in favor of "eradicated." You will be pleased to know that no one accused our students directly of wanton destruction. But, in retrospect, it should be obvious to everyone that when you cram upwards of two thousand people into a hall designed for five hundred, the occasional beaker is bound to get broken. And when this is allowed to happen for an extended period of time — for instance until the police arrive — it is conceivable that there should be very little left of eighty-two projects. Thus, we are now the first school which, upon placing its first entry after a long leave of absence, is emphatically invited never to return. Oh, yes, it's also nice to know that, in the face of adversity, our staff can be depended on to react with efficiency and calm. "Let he who is without sin cast the first bucket of blue water." That's all. Have a good day.

Mr. Morrison sat at his desk, acting extremely nonchalant, and making no comment about the announcement. He examined his fingernails and racked his brain for something to say that did not relate to the previous day's happenings, in which he had played such a major role.

Sheldon and Paul sat at their desks holding a spontaneous contest over who would be first to break out laughing. Paul had resolved to treat the matter grimly, but one look at Sheldon's face dissipated his intentions on the spot.

Wayne-o stood up. "Mr. Morrison, I want to say that you were just great yesterday, standing up for Mike like you did."

Mr. Morrison flushed bright red. "It was a very foolish thing, and — "

"No it wasn't! It was amazing! What a shot! Anyway, I want you to know that I'm proud to be in your homeroom."

A burst of applause crackled in the room. Mr. Morrison didn't know whether to laugh or cry. He had disgraced himself and his school, and thereby received his first ever demonstration of student appreciation. What a muddle, but — it all felt rather good. He permitted himself a smile. That judge was an insensitive clod anyway. He deserved to be blue.

Please excuse the interruption. In all the excitement about the science fair, I neglected to mention a matter so vital that it's a wonder it slipped my mind. The girls' basketball team plays its first scheduled game against Laguna High School in exactly one week's time. Coach Murphy informs me that we have no players. This is unfortunate, since the players are often one of the deciding factors in a basketball game. Last minute tryouts will be held this afternoon after classes. That's all.

"Well, I guess we blew our big chance for glory at the science fair yesterday," said Paul as he and Sheldon headed for English class. "The girls' basketball team doesn't seem bound for greatness."

Sheldon looked thoughtful. "Oh, I don't know about that. How much do you want to bet that we win that game at Laguna?"

"Any money," grinned Paul. "We don't have any players, and even if we did, I've heard Laguna's one of the best teams in the city."

"I predict a burst of enthusiasm in basketball here at Don Carey High School."

"Oh yeah? Why?"

"Haven't you noticed lately what a keen interest Mike is taking in the sports program?" asked Sheldon innocently. "When the girls at this school find out that Mike intends to sponsor this team personally, I figure the tryouts'll be mobbed."

Warning bells went off inside Paul's head. "Aw, Shel, you don't have the nerve to do that again — at least not so soon after yesterday's disaster."

"Yesterday wasn't a disaster — it was a triumph. Okay, so we didn't win. But neither did anybody else. I think of the whole science fair as one big tie, which is pretty good when you consider Mike isn't used to competition like that. And no one can say we have no school spirit after that great turnout. If we can get a crowd like that at the basketball game, poor Laguna will be too psyched-out to play. And all we have to do is convince Mike to show up."

"He's bound to remember what happened yesterday and say no."

"But we know how to handle him now," argued Sheldon. "If he doesn't respond to reason, you'll just beg and grovel like you did last time. Anyway, the important thing is to get the team out this afternoon. No team, no game."

In chemistry class, Paul was taken completely off-guard when Daphne Sylvester spoke to him. This event was so unexpected that at first he was not able to take in her words. "Pardon me?"

"I said I've noticed that you and Mike Otis are pretty good friends."

"Well . . . uh . . . I guess so," Paul stammered warily.

Daphne's normally vacant eyes assumed a dreamy expression. "Is he really as wonderful as everyone says he is?"

"Oh yes," Paul choked. "He's wonderful all right."

"What's he like?"

"He's very — intense."

Daphne sighed. "Do you think there'd be any way that I could get to — you know — *meet* him?"

Well, this was typical. Here he was, the lab partner of the most beautiful girl in the school. Since Day One, he had been secretly dying for even the tiniest bit of her attention. Now, finally, she speaks to him for the first time all year, and it turns out that she's making a play for Mike Otis. *Mike Otis!*

His first impulse was to say, "He's married," but he fought it down. By rights, he should alert Mike to this situation, for surely even Mike could not fail to notice the attractions of the divine Daphne. But then there were the hard feelings. The world was such a complicated place that he could not be expected to spend his time improving the quality of life for others. But if she found Mike beyond her fair reach, would she not then naturally try for his right-hand man, good old Paul Abrams? Realistically, no. However, the spirit of Steve was a powerful weapon to use on someone who looked so much like a leading lady. And the spirit of Steve pointed to the greater glory of Don't Care High.

"Well, the best way to get Mike's attention is to get involved. For example, Mike's really into the basketball team. Why don't you try out?"

"Mike supports the team?"

"Personally," Paul confirmed. "He's really excited about next Tuesday's game at Laguna."

Daphne flashed him a smile that turned his knees to water. Then she became thoughtful as she gave him the signal to begin the experiment.

With a huge sigh, Paul sorted the equipment. The divine Daphne may have shown enthusiasm for Mike Otis, but it certainly hadn't changed her attitude toward lab work.

In the three lunch periods, Sheldon passed the word about Mike's sudden interest in the basketball team, and so by the later periods of the day, the hearts and minds of the student body of Don Carey High School had completed the transition from sewers to hoops.

Not so the staff, however. And so, in the final period, Mr. Willis, who had always believed sarcasm to be a legitimate outlet for his frustrations, and whose sprained ankle was acting up again, couldn't resist saying,

"Well, Mike, that was quite an impressive showing you and your followers made at the science fair." He chuckled. "I guess you're really 'flushed with pride' about the whole business."

Mike, who was not easily perturbed, simply nodded. Although Paul felt his feathers ruffled a little, he said nothing.

"That's all in the past anyway," put in Trudy Helfield. "The basketball team is the big thing now." She turned and looked directly at Mike. "I intend to try out right after class."

Paul cast a glance in Mike's direction. The ex-president's black eyes had grown veiled and wary. It seemed as though Mike was developing a sixth sense to detect the beginnings of things he didn't understand that would haunt him just the same. Finally, Mike said, "That's nice," whereupon every girl in the class over five-foot-four pledged that she, too, would be there at the tryouts.

"Might we do a little photography?" suggested Mr. Willis. "I'm sorry, but I need to every now and then, because it makes me feel so useful."

Wayne-o strolled into the room. "Hey, Mr. Willis, what's up?"

"Sit down, Wayne. We have a lot of work to do today."

When the class was out, Paul headed directly home, not wanting to be around as the entire female population of the school converged on the bug-eyed Coach Murphy to vie for a position on the now-famous basketball team. When he got home, his mother greeted him at the door with a newspaper clipping which she shoved under his nose. The headline read: DON'T CARE STUDENTS ZOO SCIENCE FAIR.

Underneath, it said: 82 PROJECTS DESTROYED AS LETHARGIC SCHOOL AWAKENS.

"Paul, what's going on at this school of yours?"

"It was just a little misunderstanding. I don't really know much about it."

"Oh? Well then, how come you're mentioned in this article? By name, as one of the personal confidantes of Mike Otis. I want you to stay away from this Mike Otis. He sounds like a roughneck to me."

Paul laughed out loud. "Look, Mom, it's a good school. The people there have more spirit than anyone I've ever seen. And as for Mike, he did a science project, and now he's turning his attention to the basketball team. Some roughneck. I suppose the next time I turn around, you'll be accusing Tinkerbell of homicide."

On Monday, Paul turned sixteen. This occasion was marked by a special dinner at Auntie Nancy's house and the ceremonial doing of the dishes, pointing out the fact that there was no dishwasher on the premises. Auntie Nancy also presented Paul with a flashy designer shirt, which he decided to put away until his next visit to Edmondo.

Although Paul had tried to conceal his birthday, Sheldon had gotten wind of it, and bought Paul a double album entitled *The Door Fell Off Our Bus: Flash Flood selects the 23 greatest rock songs since eternity.* In addition, various cards and gifts arrived by mail from assorted relatives sprinkled across the continent.

Surprisingly, the most enthusiastic birthday celebrant was Paul's father. Canceling meetings by the score, he saw to it that he was home on Monday to greet the birthday boy and usher him into adulthood personally. He presented Paul with an electric shaver, not at all concerned by the fact that his son, as yet, had grown nothing worth shaving. Then, his eyes sparkling with pride, Mr. Abrams pulled out a brand-new copy of *The Driver's Handbook*, and announced that he intended to have Paul behind the wheel of a car inside of two weeks.

For his part, Paul tried to look enthusiastic, and submitted patiently to his father's energetic lectures on the ways of the road. For some reason, he had lost most of his burning ambition to drive. In Saskatoon, driving was a lot more important because everything was so flat and spread out, and the buses came once in a blue moon. But here in Manhattan, practically everything was within walking distance — or at least subway distance — and the most important transportation vehicle was an elevator.. Besides, traffic was always at a standstill, there were never any parking spaces on the street, and the public garages all charged five thousand dollars a minute. And since he never left New York anyway, his life as a licensed driver was going to be exactly the same as when he had been a mere child of fifteen.

Nonetheless, Paul could still hear his father raving to his mother long after Paul had headed to his room to go to sleep. While Mr. Abrams described the perfect left turn in the living room, Paul knelt at his window, scanning the building across the street for signs of Rabbit Man. With all the excitement at school, he hadn't really been keeping up to date on the apartments across the way, and here were the consequences. For all he knew, Rabbit Man may have decided to make his warren elsewhere, for his windows were dark, the shades drawn.

Not only that, but the fire-eater now wore heavy bandages on his lower lip. There was a message there somewhere, Paul was certain, about practice not always making perfect.

A new attraction had surfaced a few floors below the fire-eater. The world's ultimate football fan had moved in, and when he was not glued to the TV screen watching pro, college, Canadian, and even high school games, he was hard at work ripping up his carpets and laying down Astroturf. It was impossible to see the rest of the apartment, but the part near the window was done up as the end zone of the Orange Bowl.

The people next door weren't watching their set, so Steve had the night off.

He finally drifted off to sleep to the sounds of his father talking about parallel parking.

At school, Coach Murphy was in a state of unparalleled joy. Not only would he be able to produce five players on Thursday afternoon, but he had a first team, a second team, and substitutes. And enthusiasm! The girls had volunteered to put in two hours a day after school, plus individual practice at home, and had even worked out over the weekend. Oh, he had definitely died and gone to heaven! Of course, he did realize that the only reason for this burst of support was an inexplicable decision on the part of Mike Otis to have this team win. But Coach Murphy didn't share the cynicism of his fellow teachers, especially Mr. Gamble. An opportunity like this was to be exploited at all costs, regardless of its source. As far as Coach was concerned, Mike Otis could wear a raincoat as big as Chicago and stick safety pins in his nostrils, so long as he kept supporting the sports program.

On Tuesday, Sheldon and Paul managed to extract a vague promise from Mike to attend the Laguna game. It took quite a bit of begging and pleading, but not as much as Paul had anticipated it would after the science fair. Mike gave in with a kind of bland graciousness, as he had apparently accepted the fact that he had certain duties to this public he had so mysteriously acquired. He was sure that it was all related to some basic idea which was included among the many things at this school that he didn't understand.

"I know how to handle him now," Sheldon said afterwards as the two left the building. "I just let you do the talking. It works like a charm."

"Why me?"

"Because you're nice, Ambition. Not flashy, and you certainly don't have a silver tongue like mine. But Mike doesn't respond to reason anyway. He responds to your natural inherent niceness."

Paul wasn't sure just how to take this. On the surface, it was a compliment, but Sheldon's use of the word *nice* seemed ever so slightly tainted. The expression "Nice guys finish last" kept cropping up in his mind, and Paul couldn't seem to remember any of those late movies counting *nice* among the many attributes of Steve.

"Anyway," Sheldon went on, "the basketball game is practically in the bag. We've covered all the angles. And it occurs to me that since it's barely four o'clock, this would be an excellent time to sample some Mexican cuisine. Did you know that there's a great Mexican place not too far from Don't Care High?"

"No, and I think I'd like to live a little longer before the great secret is revealed to me. Honestly, Shel, my stomach has just recovered from that stupid souvlaki you forced down my throat last time."

"Come on," scoffed Sheldon. "Tell your stomach to follow me, and we'll really see what it's made of."

That evening, despite paralyzing stomach pains brought on by three possibly-tainted enchiladas, Paul passed the written examination to earn his beginning driver's permit. Mr. Abrams treated this as the equivalent of a victory at the Indianapolis 500.

"All those other test candidates had no idea what they were doing, but you were great!"

"But everyone passed."

"There's a difference between just getting by and knowing what you're doing. You knew what you were doing." He then dismissed the many drivers' education programs available to students, and reiterated his intention of teaching his son personally.

"Gee, thanks, Dad," said Paul weakly. He'd had no complaints against New York recently, but here was one. These streets were patrolled by lunatics, bumper to bumper. A person should learn to drive in a sane place — like, oh, let's say, Saskatoon. He could accept that this was a very unStevelike sentiment, because Steve always knew in advance that he would emerge unscathed driving through the mine field, the landslide, and the washed-out bridge. But since no one had provided Paul with a copy of the script, it was fairly obvious that he would drive a quarter of a block, and then four fleets of taxis would appear from nowhere and grind him into a thin layer of dust over the bike lane. He sighed. Considering the insanity that was going on at school, the career of Paul Abrams, driver extraordinaire, was a needless complication.

And as the practices raged on and basketball fever took over Don Carey, Paul allowed himself to forget about driving and concentrated on Mike Otis. Maybe it was his being mentioned in the paper as one of Mike's confidantes, or Daphne's notice of him as a good friend of Mike's, or possibly his and Sheldon's general reputations as the ex-president's main men, but Paul felt the need to get closer to Mike. His attempts were unsuccessful, as they had always been in the past. Concessions could be gained and promises extracted, but the man himself remained a complete mystery.

Still, despite his knowledge of Mike's strange circumstances, his suspicious political career and rise to power, and his off-beat personality, Paul felt that Mike was someone special. In the words of Peter Eversleigh, Mike really was "the main dude."

Finally, Paul knew he wanted to *win* on Thursday.

11

Laguna High laughed when it heard that Don Carey had put together a team and was going to dare to bring it over on Thursday. The Laguna Student Council had dispatched a letter to the students of Don't Care High which included the passage:

". . . We urge you to keep your team home, as cruelty to animals is distasteful to us. We have also heard that you place great faith in a person named Mike Otis, and we have obtained a picture of him. By the time this letter arrives, we may have stopped laughing. . . ."

"It's an outrage!" Sheldon howled in the cafeteria. "And that's why we want everybody to be there!

Everybody! We'll show them how a *real* school sticks together behind its team and its true leader!"

So, on the day of the big game, students did not even visit their lockers after class. Some headed for subways, some for private cars, and some started out on foot.

At exactly three forty-five, the principal of Laguna High became edgy as he watched the influx of Don Carey students swarm past his window, heading for the attractive, modern sports complex. He called together his staff in an emergency meeting, ordering them all to stay to act as security for the game.

"These are the monsters who leveled the science fair. How can we know how they'll react when our team starts slaughtering them? So nobody goes home until they're gone."

The Laguna sports complex was the best high school facility in the city, and seated almost three thousand around the basketball court. This was ideal, as Sheldon, who had developed a great love for large numbers, estimated a twenty-four hundred-plus turnout. There were ninety Laguna teachers and about twice as many students. Don Carey's staff representation consisted of Mr. Morrison and an incredibly nervous Coach Murphy.

Outnumbered thirteen to one, the Laguna students were a subdued lot, but so were the Don't Care students, who seemed to be losing their sense of purpose in this foreign building because Mike had not yet arrived. Sheldon and Paul staked out the entrances, waiting for the president to put in an appearance. Come game time, Mike was not there.

Like its fans, the Don't Care basketball team was having a crisis of motivation. Though its practice was evident, and Daphne Sylvester was easily the tallest girl on the court, the strong Laguna team was all over them. When it became obvious that the home team was in control, the Laguna fans allowed themselves to come alive, and Paul could see that the Don't Care students, unused to participating in extracurricular activities, were becoming extremely uncomfortable. By the end of the first quarter, Laguna held a commanding 28–12 lead. And then Paul saw the shiny black behemoth nosing its way onto the sports complex parking lot.

"Shel! Shel, he's here!"

Sheldon wasted no time. As Mike got out of his car, he took off for the announcer's booth. Opening the door with a mighty kick, he grabbed the microphone from the startled announcer just as the second quarter was about to get under way. As Paul escorted Mike into the stands area, Sheldon's voice rang through the complex.

"We would now like to welcome a dignitary in the audience: the once and future president and true leader of Don't Care High — *Mike Otis*!"

Pandemonium broke loose. There was a roar so loud that the Laguna staff wondered if the structure was strong enough to handle the vibrations. All the Don't Care students were on their feet cheering, and Slim Kroy marched back and forth behind the players' bench, blasting out his now-familiar *Mike Otis Tuba Solo*. The Don't Care players just stared at Mike intently, for they were way behind in this game, and knew that Mike deserved far better than that.

Paul convinced Mike to wave, which he did in an offhand manner, and the crowd went crazy for five minutes.

Finally, order was restored, and the game resumed. But it was a new Don't Care team that faced the Laguna champions. Everything was in perspective now, and everyone's purpose was crystal clear: Mike wanted this game, and they would hand it to him or die trying.

Cheered, screamed, and oompahed on by their half-crazed fans, Daphne and her team fairly exploded. They were all over the court, lunging, weaving, dribbling, and passing as though their lives depended on it. They made up six points before their shocked opponents had a chance to gather themselves together. Then the powerful Laguna offense struck back. But Don't Care held fast, and the game became no-holds-barred, end-to-end action. The cheers were deafening as the Don't Care team fought to close the gap between themselves and Laguna.

"Hey, wait a minute!" The referee called a special team foul on Don Carey because all the LaPaz triplets were wearing the number 3. The clock was stopped, and a lively debate ensued. Finally, when the foul appeared on the scoreboard, Mr. Morrison, overwhelmed with the excitement of the situation, shot off the bench like a jet-propelled projectile, and began hurling abuse at the referee. In the end, Laguna was awarded two shots, and Mr. Morrison was ejected from the building in disgrace. Shirley and Rose LaPaz were forced to change their numbers with white tape to 33 and 333 respectively, and the tuba told the general public what Don't Care thought of the matter.

"Rip-off!" howled Sheldon in hysterics.

Paul said nothing. All his energy was concentrated on the drama that was unfolding on the court.

The battle raged on as Laguna fought to hold its lead under the staggering Don't Care attack. By halftime, the lead had been cut down to seven points, but in the third quarter, Laguna came out with everything it had and widened the lead to ten. The fourth quarter was do or die for Don't Care High. The sound was an uninterrupted roar from over twenty-four hundred throats as Arthur Morrison paced back and forth in the parking lot, biting his nails in anxiety.

Daphne and her team came out flying, and it became obvious that Don't Care had the power edge this quarter as Laguna began to look tired. But the question remained: Would they have the time?

Slowly but surely, the lead dropped from ten to eight to six. With a minute and a half left, the score was 61–57, but then a Trudy Helfield interception brought Don't Care High to within two. Then Daphne Sylvester fouled, and one successful shot brought the Laguna lead to three, with forty-five seconds to play. As the seconds ticked away, Don't Care thundered down the court, but when the ball passed through the hoop, bringing them within one, there were only twelve seconds remaining on the clock.

The Laguna team began to pass the ball around to kill time, but from nowhere leaped Daphne Sylvester, who smacked the ball away in midair, whereupon it passed through the hands of all three LaPazes, then to Trudy Helfield and through the hoop a split second before the buzzer went off, ending the game. Final score: 63—62, Don Carey.

There was a moment of absolute dead silence as the buzzer rang. Suddenly, Mr. Morrison burst in from the parking lot door, ran out onto the court, looked up at the scoreboard, and let fly with a joyous, inarticulate howl. Then Sheldon's estimated twenty-four hundred-plus crowd went absolutely berserk.

Sheldon and Paul both rode in the ambulance with Peter Eversleigh, who was being taken to the local emergency room, suffering from super-severe indigestion.

"Oh, dudes! Oh, dudes, dudes, dudes!" Peter kept groaning to Sheldon and Paul, who watched in concern. "This tournament which we have just witnessed was one of the most conceptual experiences of my life! I was so nervous that I didn't even know I was doing it!"

"How much of that licorice did you eat?" asked Paul.

"My whole week's supply of stick, dude. Sixty-seven long ones. Ohhh! My stomach feels so neg, I can hardly conceptualize."

"Take it easy," Sheldon counseled. "The doctor says you'll be fine."

"I want to relay my gratitude to you dudes for riding with me and leaving the celebration." He shuddered. "I've got to give up stick. After today, this is a confection from which I will keep my distance."

At the hospital, the doctors told Sheldon and Paul that Peter would not need his stomach pumped, and that it was just a massive case of indigestion due to indiscreet eating of licorice. He was to rest for an hour, and then they could take him home.

Sheldon relaxed in his chair in the waiting room. "Ah, Ambition, what could be more perfect than this day?"

"I can think of a lot of things," said Paul wearily. "The win was beautiful, but it would be nice if the Laguna sports building was still standing."

"Stop exaggerating. When the section of stands collapsed, I admit I was a little worried. But even the Laguna students cheered, because that part needed rebuilding anyway. And our people only tore down one basket."

"And how about when Slim bopped their student council president on the head with his tuba?"

Sheldon shrugged. "It was an accident, and the guy was a creep to begin with. And don't forget, Mr. Morrison made an official apology to their staff for any damages we might have caused."

"Yes, but it would have been nice if he'd kept a straight face while he was doing it. I don't think the principal was too impressed when he kept cracking up. I doubt if a giggled-out apology is enough for the stands, the basket, all the scuffs and scrapes we put on the floor when we mobbed the court, and all the bushes and flowers that got trampled when they threw us out of the building. Let's face it, it was exactly like the science fair."

"Only this time we won," Sheldon added.

Paul smiled in spite of himself.

By the time Peter Eversleigh was safely home and Paul had returned to his apartment, he was late for dinner, which he knew would bring about a certain amount of cross-examination.

"Paul, where have you been? It's so late."

"Oh, sorry, Mom. Sheldon and I were with a sick friend."

"Thank goodness!" his mother breathed. "I thought you were at that dreadful basketball game they're talking about on the radio."

Paul inhaled deeply. "Actually, that's where Peter got sick. He kind of overdid it on licorice."

"You mean you were at that awful game? Oh, Paul! On the radio they announced that the Don Carey students caused a riot!"

"It was a peaceful game," Paul insisted. "We won it fair and square. Granted, a few things did get broken, but it was all unintentional, and it certainly wasn't anything close to being a riot."

All throughout dinner, Mrs. Abrams bewailed the "horrible school" Paul attended and the "bad crowd" he had fallen in with. The term "wanton destruction" came up a lot, too, and the name "Mike Otis" was spat out as though it were "Attila the Hun."

Mr. Abrams offered up the "We're not in the

boonies anymore" explanation, but this time his wife shot it down handily.

"Mom, please don't knock Mike so much. If there's one thing that's absolutely true here, it's that none of this is Mike's fault." Paul pushed away his half-eaten dinner. "I'm really not very hungry. I'm going to my room."

Sitting down on his bed, he frowned. Don't Care High certainly seemed to be developing a reputation across the city if its exploits had managed to reach even his mother's sedate radio station, where the most exciting news stories were fifty percent-off sales on tomatoes and cantaloupes. Was the school's reputation deserved? Well, certainly the damage reports were accurate. But nobody seemed to *understand*. The whole Otis revolution was so special, yet it was getting such a bad name.

Absently, he switched on his clock radio in time to hear the voice of Flash Flood annouce, "Well, it's seven-fifteen in the greatest city in the world, but you wouldn't know it by looking at the traffic. Parking lots on all major routes. The weather — it looks like we'll be able to put off that first frost for a few more weeks. And so the forecast is hot, and will remain hot for the duration of our brand-new garbage strike, giving way to severe blizzard activity once the smell dies down.

"Okay, this next song goes out to Mike Otis and the students of Don't Care High, who've been *very busy* lately, in case you haven't heard. With a wrecked science fair already to their credit, today they battered the Laguna basketball team, and after that they battered Laguna. Damage estimates are right up there, and who can tell what's next for the fearless fighters of the Sewerman's School? I just hope they don't come to Stereo 99, 'cause this building can hardly stand up on its own."

Paul ignored the undertones and listened with an obvious swelling of pride. Mike Otis had put Don't Care High on the map.

As always, Flash Flood was right. The weather remained hot, and the garbage piled up all over the city. It was a time of mellowing for Don't Care High, and the students floated in the gentle euphoria brought on their triumph over Laguna and their true leader, whom they revered regardless of whether or not he held the official title of president.

Staff spirits were improving as well. The administration was not too pleased with having to hand over reparations to Laguna and the Midtown Community Center, but Mr. Gamble preached a "Never cry over spilt milk" philosophy, and the incidents were thus smoothed over. Anticipating a long period of calm, the vice-principal looked ten years younger.

Even Mr. Willis seemed to be on the road to recovery. His sprained ankle was finally beginning to heal after complications had set in and, even though he still had problems, they were problems with photography. This was fair, he felt, since it was covered under his job description.

Peter Eversleigh swore off licorice for life, which he claimed was the best decision he had ever made, as he felt he was now more capable than ever of appreciating the conceptuality that blossomed all around him. He had taken to chewing gum, and spent a lot of his time with Rosalie Gladstone, the expert.

Wayne-o was developing a real rapport with Mr. Morrison, which was surprising the two of them. Wayne-o was so impressed with Mr. Morrison's temper tantrum and subsequent ejection over the LaPaz foul at the basketball game that he took time out to congratulate him in homeroom. He even took a picture of him for photography class, which he entitled "Wayne-o's Homeroom Teacher."

The only casualty of the transformation of Don't Care High was the man who had once held a near-monopoly on the crumbling halls of that institution. Feldstein had never quite recovered from the failure of his locker ban, had never quite believed his eyes when "The Sewer System" had grown and flourished in the midst of the strongest sanctions he had ever imposed. It was inconceivable that such an effort could possibly have taken place under such rigid locker restrictions. And yet the mysterious power of Mike Otis had won the day.

Many hours Feldstein sat in his chair, contemplating the demise of the locker business and racking his brain trying to penetrate the secret of the man who, to this day, still kept 205C from him. He watched his old enemies, the guys from The Combo, and even his archnemesis, Slim Kroy — all people he had ruthlessly forced out of the business — flourishing under Mike Otis. One thing was clear. Under the Otis regime, the economic climate of the school was not healthy for the locker game. There would be no more deals in his future, just a deserted stairwell, a stockpile of 263 accumulated favors, and eventually an empty chair.

Feldstein's predicament was not immediately noticeable, however, as something far more distracting was in the works. Daphne Sylvester had started an all-out campaign to bring herself to the attention of Mike Otis. The divine Daphne was experimenting with every conceivable kind of fashion, hairstyle, and makeup, which was having no effect on Mike, but was turning Paul and the rest of the male population of Don't Care High prematurely gray. Paul's chemistry grade was in a nose dive, which he felt was important, but not quite so important as the direct threat on his life Daphne's new campaign posed. Powerful acids and bases would fly in all directions, and even poisonous gas would be ignored when Daphne selected a new miniskirt. Mike was completely unmoved.

Even Sheldon was impressed. "I'll tell you, Ambition, I can accept that Mike is the way he is, and comes from a family so normal you could die. I can handle his car and his clothes. But when I see Daphne throwing herself at him, and him not even looking at her — that's living proof that he's not human!"

"Yeah, well, count your blessings," said Paul feelingly. "I'm her new strategy consultant. She's having this big confidence crisis, and every day in chemistry I get to hear about it. She's modeling for me, saying, 'Do you think this'll get his attention?' Shel, if this keeps up, I'm going to be the first person in history ever to die of someone else's broken heart!"

Nor did Paul's high blood pressure have a chance to subside outside of school hours. Before he knew it, the weekend was upon him and his father had scheduled his first driving lesson.

They started out bright and early Saturday with Mr. Abrams behind the wheel and Paul watching attentively. This was demonstration time, after which the drivers would switch. Mr. Abrams soon found out that demonstrations were difficult in New York City, especially if they were executed slowly and carefully for teaching purposes. His left turn was marred when two taxis sped past him through the yellow light; his right turn lost its finesse when two men wheeled an eleven-foot clothing rack out in front of the car. The freeway lesson landed them in a traffic jam where the maximum speed attained was eight miles per hour. And parking was left out altogether because they could not find a spot. Mr. Abrams was becoming visibly upset. His commentary was much more colorful than was his habit, and he categorized all other drivers as "idiots," "maniacs," and "grannies." Finally, they found a street which Mr. Abrams deemed suitable, and Paul took over the wheel.

Never before had Paul heard so many car horns honk at once. Never before had he seen such a blur of yellow as taxis passed him on all sides. And never before had he seen his father so serene.

"Don't worry about him, son. He's just an idiot. You're doing fine. Just concentrate on what you're doing. Remember your lane. That's it. Watch that maniac. Good. Don't worry. If he had time to honk, he had time to get out of the way. Don't worry."

Paul drove for the better part of an hour, then they switched again, and Mr. Abrams scratched the car.

"What a stupid place to put a mailbox!" he seethed, his serenity gone. "It's practically in the middle of the road! You'd think the government would have better things to do than to create hazards for ordinary citizens!"

It was Paul's turn to be serene. "Don't worry, Dad." Nothing could spoil his exhilaration. He had operated a motor vehicle in New York City, and he was still alive. Even Steve could make no greater claim.

12

New York's garbage strike raged on. A mountain of refuse sprouted up in front of Paul's building, the accumulated cast-offs of forty stories of people. Pedestrian traffic, cramped at best, was now even more difficult as people had to thread their way among walls of overstuffed bags. True to Flash Flood's prediction, the weather stayed unseasonably warm, and a smell hung in the air which Sheldon took to calling "the funk of forty thousand years."

Don't Care High was relatively calm, which Paul interpreted as good. But Sheldon was becoming restless.

"I'm telling you, Ambition, no good can come of this," he declared one morning before homeroom. "There's absolutely nothing happening. These people need a cause, or pretty soon the whole 'don't care' thing will be back again. We can't let this go on too long. We're playing with fire here."

"We're not playing with fire," Paul explained patiently. "You see, this is called peace. It's that funny thing that fills in the holes between catastrophes. I like it."

Sheldon shook his head vehemently. "Too much of this and the whole school will be out to lunch again. It's time to get everybody all riled up."

Paul groaned. "About what?"

Sheldon shook his head. "It's so obvious — Mike is our true leader. He's led us through the science fair. He's led us through the basketball game. But he's still not reinstated as student body president. Don't you see? We've been so happy with our achievements that we've overlooked the real issue. There is a great wrong that we still haven't righted."

"Shel, you're getting that look on your face again," said Paul unhappily.

Sheldon ignored him. "Yes! We were off the track for a while, but now it's time to get Mike back into office. We settled things on the outside; now we're going to settle them on the inside. We owe it to Mike."

"We don't owe Mike anything except a lot of peace and quiet! This has nothing to do with Mike! You're just looking to stir things up! So whatever you're planning, *forget it*!"

* * *

May I have your attention, please. There is only one announcement. The staff is once again accepting nominations for the office of student body president. Isn't it odd how this seems to happen so often? That's all. Have a good day.

In the groundswell of confusion, Paul Abrams leaped to his feet, his face flaming. *"What?"*

Mr. Morrison looked uncomfortable. "Well, you see — "

"They're trying to replace Mike!" cried Paul.

As those words sunk in, a murmur of hostility ran around the room.

"But they can't do that!"

"That's not possible!"

Wayne-o burst in the door. "Hold it! Hold everything! Something weird's going on! Mr. Morrison, what's all this about a new president?"

"Well, Wayne, it's like this — "

"How can we let this happen after all Mike did for us?" shouted Paul, as Sheldon sat passively by, marveling at how his planned rekindling of interest had started so effortlessly. "We've been so happy with our victories that we've forgotten Mike's still out of office!"

"Not for long!" shouted Dan Wilburforce.

"Uh, kids," said Mr. Morrison, "could I just say something — "

"We want Mike back!" screamed a LaPaz, possibly Rose.

"Just a minute, everybody," said Mr. Morrison,

wishing he could find a way to join the protest without having Gamble murder him. "I sympathize with your problems. I was there at the science fair and the basketball game, so I know exactly how you feel about Mike. But just remember one thing: The administration of this school has just had to give money for damages to the Midtown Community Center and Laguna High so everyone in the office is in a very bad mood concerning Mike Otis. I believe you should be able to voice your opinions, but I'm not in charge. Be very, very careful. I don't want to see any of you suspended or expelled."

After homeroom, it became apparent that the discontent was general. Students were once again upset that Mike was out of office. Paul, who had lashed out at Sheldon not a half hour earlier for precisely the same thoughts, was thinking revolution. Rebellious voices rang in the halls.

Now Sheldon was preaching moderation. "Morrison's right. Gamble must be ready to hang anybody who steps out of line on Mike's behalf. We're going to have to stay within the rules."

"How are we going to do that?" Paul asked.

"I don't know," said Sheldon. "We have to figure out some way to remind all the teachers that we still support Mike, but we can't get too pushy or Gamble will be all over us like a blanket. We can't risk a poster campaign — not after the last one. We have to stay completely within the rules and, at the same time, let the staff know that when they take a breath in this school, they're breathing Otis air." The two entered English class.

As they took their seats, Paul pondered the problem at hand: how to remind the teachers that the issue was still alive. He watched as Miss Vlorque entered the room, shuffled some papers, and looked as though she were about to begin the lesson. And suddenly the answer seemed so simple. He leaped to his feet and announced,

"Excuse me, Miss Vlorque. Before we start, I'd like to say something on behalf of the class. We want you to know that we all support Mike Otis, and we think that it's terribly unjust that he isn't student body president right now."

Sheldon began to clap, not madly, but steadily, and the class joined in. There was no hooting or hollering, just an earnest round of polite applause indicating approval of Paul's words. When the sedate ovation ended, Paul said,

"Thank you for listening," and sat back down.

A confused Miss Vlorque glanced at Paul strangely and then began her lesson.

"Ambition, you may not be a genius like me," Sheldon said once the class was dismissed, "but every now and then you have a way of cutting right to the heart of the matter. That little ceremony was perfect. Perfect! What do you want to bet it catches on?"

"I think it could catch on with a little help," agreed Paul with a grin.

"Good," said Sheldon. "I'll give it a whirl in my next class, and you try again. After a couple of weeks of this, the teachers will be begging Mike to return to office just to shut us up. And the beautiful thing is it's all so polite!"

Paul did it again in second period, with similar

results. A nice short speech, peaceful and restrained applause, and a thoroughly bewildered Mr. Schmidt.

The technique was easily passed along. Politeness was the only watchword. Students who had witnessed one of Paul's two opening performances began to try it on their own, and the three lunch periods brought about a vast pooling of information. During those three hours, the word spread like wildfire, and in the last periods of the day, classes all over the school were started off by a student spontaneously pledging support to Mike Otis.

"Don't even bother to mention this new president thing," Sheldon advised a group who had come to him for advice. "We don't recognize that. Just remember — be polite."

In photography, Paul was reluctant to go through the exercise with Mike present, not to mention Mr. Willis, who had sprained his ankle over an eight-by-ten glossy of that same Mike. But Trudy Helfield stood up.

"I beg your pardon, Mr. Willis, but before we start, I think it should be said that everyone in this room supports Mike Otis and feels it's unfair that he's not allowed to be president." During the applause, Trudy shot Mike a dazzling smile. Mike gazed out the window with great concentration.

Mr. Willis leaned on his crutches, a disgusted expression on his face.

"So, Mr. Otis, whatever did you do to earn such loyalty from these fine fellow students of yours?"

"I didn't do anything," said Mike blandly.

"No," said Mr. Willis. "Of course you didn't. And

now, if no one minds, we can begin — "

Wayne-o came bursting in the door. "Am I late?"

"Not as much as usual," sighed Mr. Willis. "Take a seat, Wayne."

"Okay, but before I do, I'd like to say something on behalf of the class. You see, we all support — "

"We've been through all that, Wayne, including the applause."

Wayne-o looked hurt. "Darn," he said mildly, and took his chair.

By the middle of the next week, the preclass pledge of support to Mike Otis had become a full-blown custom. Not a single hour would begin without the traditional benediction and applause, and any student at all could be expected to do the honors. There was no predicting who would be the one in any given class, as the duty was passed around freely and assumed by spontaneous inspiration.

Paul could see that the ritual was more than grating on his teachers' nerves. Miss Vlorque in particular faced each morning with the dread usually reserved for a mugging: She knew what would happen, but she didn't know when and from whom. Mr. Schmidt had taken to lurking outside the classroom in the hope of missing the exercise. This did not work. His students always waited for him. Once he even stayed away so long that Wayne-o was already in class when he arrived. Wayne-o suggested that the teacher be marked absent. The irritable Mr. Schmidt was not amused. Mr. Willis had taken to reciting the pledge along with the current speaker, usually adding "Yeah, yeah, yeah! We know already!" at appropriate intervals. The students were unperturbed; Mr. Willis, on the other hand, was operating on an increasingly short fuse.

Sheldon was delighted. "If you live long enough, Ambition, you learn something new every day," he said philosophically. "Who would have believed that simple courtesy could be such a powerful weapon? It's driving them nuts! I've got a history teacher whose whole face contorts every time we do our thing. Yesterday Mr. Hennessey lost control for a minute and shouted 'If one more person thanks me for listening, I'll —' before he caught himself. So we thanked him for listening. It was inspirational."

"I'm getting a little worried about poor Mr. Willis, though," said Paul. "It's starting to look as though he's going to freak out one day and never freak back in again. Maybe we should skip doing it in his class."

"No compromises. This thing is really working. It's like when you keep putting spoonfuls of sugar into a cup of coffee. Eventually it comes out tasting like diesel fuel."

Throughout all these goings-on, Feldstein sat in his stairwell, tight-lipped and unforgiving, waiting for the end. His ill humor had stimulated his appetite, and he was using up his stockpile of favors at an alarming rate. If there was one thing that characterized this phase of Don't Care history besides the Mike Otis speeches, it was the scores of students called temporarily away from their normal lives to carry trays of food into the locker baron's stairwell.

The situation was becoming so alarming that even Sheldon paused from his speech campaign to take notice. He tried to talk to Feldstein, but the locker baron was implacable.

"I can't believe this is happening!" Sheldon told Paul as the two walked through the halls after Sheldon's meeting with Feldstein. "I can't believe that Feldstein has come to this! Do you realize that last week he called in *ninety* favors? He just sits there like a big blob of nothing, sucking back food like a vacuum cleaner. He's already gained weight — they say that's how it happened to Slim Kroy."

"You never see him now without food," Paul agreed. "And a lot of the kids are getting hit for old favors — Wayne-o, Phil, Rosalie, Samuel. He hit the LaPazes three times."

Sheldon sighed. "When a great man comes along, the old order changeth. Feldstein came into a school that was in locker anarchy, and he brought the whole ball of wax under one roof and wiped out the competition. But no one stays on top forever."

As they continued to walk, they came upon Peter Eversleigh sitting by his locker, looking somehow naked without his customary stick of licorice.

Paul nudged Sheldon. "Look at his collar."

Attached to the collar of Peter's shirt was a large safety pin.

"Hey, Peter," Sheldon called, "is that holding your head on?"

"Symbolism," said Peter humorlessly, snapping his gum in the Rosalie Gladstone style. "This pin of which we speak is a reflection of the pins worn by our main dude, Mike Otis, on the cuffs of his pants.

With this pin I am making my own statement on the bogus concept of the exile of our leader. It shows that I support the dude."

Sheldon's and Paul's eyes met. Simultaneously, calculating grins spread over their faces.

"I'd say that's conceptual, wouldn't you say so, Ambition?"

"Very conceptual," Paul agreed. "Good concept."

Peter was gratified. "Thank you, dudes."

Sheldon slapped Paul on the arm. "Come on. Let's go shopping."

Within forty-eight hours, seventy-five percent of the population of Don't Care High was wearing safety pins on all shirts and blouses. There were small ones and large ones, and all sizes in between, ranging right up to kilt pin size. And the trend was still growing. Pinned students would come across unpinned friends in the halls and rush them out to nearby stores lest they give the impression that they were not in support of Mike. Others still kept extras on hand for the less enlightened.

By the following week, virtually all the students wore pins religiously every day. Peter Eversleigh, on the grounds that he was the creator of the whole thing, wore two pins. So did Wayne-o, on grounds he would not explain. The LaPazes wore three each, and that they didn't have to explain. No one would wear the large, plastic-tipped diaper kind, as that was reserved for Mike himself.

Sheldon picked a sporty model, large and shiny silver, while Paul stuck with a sedate but tasteful one-inch pin.

The pins showed exactly how popular Mike really

was. A bare collar was a great rarity among the students, and this visual representation of the incredible support for Mike inspired people all the more.

And as the days flew by, Feldstein continued to burn up favors at unbelievable speed. He now spent all his time — from nine until three-thirty — sitting in his stairwell, eating. He had moved in a few desks as waiting buffets for incoming snacks, and these were constantly laden with a wide variety of goodies. His attitude had gone from anger to depression. Down to his final thirty favors, he acted as though he knew the end was near, and he intended to go out in a wild blaze of overindulgence. The eating action was intense, and as the safety pins and speeches ruled Don't Care High, many students avoided Feldstein's stairwell, for the sight there was not pretty.

Mike Otis himself might have overlooked the entire safety pin affair had it not been for the fact that students were constantly approaching him to show off their pins. Many times Paul had seen the ex-president accosted by a student proudly displaying a gleaming new pin. There would be an awkward pause as Mike decided whether or not a comment was called for. Then he would say, "Very nice," and move on. Mike was now coming into contact with more students than ever before, and might have been moved to wonder what these safety pins had to do with him had he not been positive that it all had its place in the now-complex network of things at this school that he didn't understand. On a couple of occasions, Paul himself tried to speak with Mike. He could see the questions bubbling just below the surface of Mike's strange calm. But they were never asked, and the conversations were always brief and uncomfortable, with Mike responding to direct questions only and giving answers where brevity was exceeded only by vagueness.

As always, though, Paul was swept up in the general tide of things. The preclass exercises raged politely and mercilessly on, and the safety pin campaign continued to blanket the school. He and Sheldon were already known as Mike's top advisors and, as such, they were frequently sought out for consultation on such matters as the wording of the speech, or what type of pin to wear. So Paul was taken completely off guard when he found himself summoned to see Feldstein.

Paul poked his head timidly through the doors of Feldstein's stairwell. His jaw dropped. The slightly chubby locker baron, his face a study in melancholy, sat amidst a vast smorgasbord consisting of several trays of cold sliced meats, cole slaw, enchiladas, fifteen varieties of cheese, several loaves of bread, an enormous hot-fudge and butterscotch-quintuple-scoop banana split, and a basket of fresh fruit. Pizza cartons were stacked in the corner, right by the potato chips, and as Paul watched in amazement, two boys carried in a three-tiered, white-frosted wedding cake, complete with silver bells.

"Good news, Feldstein," called one of them. "The groom didn't show up."

Feldstein nodded wearily. "Just put it down there by the halvah."

The two boys set down the cake and hurried away.

Paul spoke up. "You wanted to see me, Feldstein?"

"You came into this school without a locker, and I got you one. Now I need a favor from you."

Paul swallowed hard. "What'll it be, Feldstein?"

Reaching around the soup tureen which simmered on the hot plate, Feldstein indicated the fruit basket. "Mangoes, man. I need mangoes. Four of them. Ripe."

"Right." Paul ran off in search of Sheldon. He found his friend in the cafeteria line. "Shel! Shel, quick! What's a mango?"

Sheldon nodded understandingly. "Feldstein called in the favor, huh? I guess we should have expected it. Well, a mango is some kind of tropical fruit. That's all I know. There are a few fruit stores around here, but they're only good for apples, oranges, and bananas."

"You'll help me, right?"

Sheldon chuckled condescendingly. "In this life, Ambition, there are some things that a man must do on his own."

Paul spread his arms in desperation, "But where am I going to get four mangoes? Will he accept, let's say, a good-sized watermelon instead?"

A hum went up in the line from the sheer absurdity of this statement.

"Feldstein doesn't acccept substitutions," explained Sheldon. "*Any* substitutions. Once I saw him turn down a bowl of soup because it came with plain crackers instead of Ritz."

Paul grimaced with determination. "I'll just have to work something out then."

"Good luck," Sheldon called after his fleeting form.

Paul made the rounds of the local fruit and grocery stores with no success. This was a mangoless neighborhood. He had known this favor would be trouble, and here it was — another insane crisis to add to that long list of insane crises he called his life. As he walked back into the school, he pondered the advisability of visiting Feldstein and admitting failure. No. He would have to come up with something that was so valuable that the locker baron would put aside his need for mangoes.

Then he saw Mike, and the answer burst upon him like a sunrise. He followed Mike to his locker, worked up his courage, and approached him.

"Hi."

A pause, then, "Hi." This was Mike's standard response to such a situation.

"Listen, Mike, I'll get right to the point. I'm in a bit of a jam, and I'd like you to do me a favor."

Mike looked wary. Such situations generally meant the beginning of something unusual. "A favor," he repeated dully.

"To be perfectly honest, I'm in the soup right now. If you do this one thing for me, I promise I'll make it up to you."

There was an excruciatingly long pause, during which time Mike looked at the ceiling, the floor, and both walls. He alternated between three distinct blank expressions. Finally, he said, "Okay."

*　*　*

"Sorry, Feldstein, I couldn't get the mangoes."

Feldstein shook his head. "He couldn't get the mangoes." His voice was not threatening, just empty.

"I got you something better," said Paul.

"No, man. That's not the way it works. You see, I need mangoes. And when I need something, there's nothing better than what I need." Feldstein stared at the combination lock Paul was holding out to him. "A lock? I've got loads of locks, man."

Paul grinned proudly. "But this one's the lock to 205C."

There was dead silence as Feldstein took this in. His eyes filled with tears. "205C?" he barely whispered.

Paul nodded.

"205C is . . . mine?"

"That's right, Feldstein. That completes your row."

Feldstein was choked with emotion. He dabbed at his eyes with the take-out menu from a local pizza parlor. Then suddenly he stood up and pushed Paul into his chair. "Here. Sit down. Have some soup. Man, this is the nicest thing anyone's ever done for me. How'd you pull it off?"

"Well," said Paul, "I just asked Mike if you could have the locker, and he said okay."

"He's a prince!" cried Feldstein. "I take back everything I said about him! I've been dumping on this whole Otis thing because I know that Slim Kroy and a lot of those guys from The Combo are mixed up in it. But now I'll do anything in my power to see to it that that great guy is president again. And you, man — I owe you! Anything!" He indicated his entire restaurant. "Chinese, Mexican, Italian — you name it! You want steak? I'm a little low, but I'll get you steak!"

"It's okay, Feldstein. It's my pleasure. Come on. Let's go complete your row."

When they reached the 200C's, Mike had cleaned out his locker and was preparing to move to his new location near the print shop. Feldstein, in a great outpouring of gratitude, ran up and embraced the slight figure in the large raincoat.

"Mike, you're the greatest! I can't tell you what this means to me!"

As soon as he was released, Mike hurried away. Although he said nothing, Paul could hear the words as clearly as if they'd been spoken: *There are a lot of things at this school I don't understand.*

A *chunk*! sound echoed through the hall, signifying that Feldstein had officially become the first figure in Don't Care locker history to control the coveted 200C series, the longest uninterrupted row of lockers in the school.

Paul felt good.

Feldstein's reluctance to support Mike had been a sobering factor on the otherwise fabulously successful Otis campaign. Within an hour of his possession of 205C, the rejuvenated locker baron managed to acquire one hundred fifty safety pins to broadcast to the world his change of heart. He threw open his delicatessen to anyone wearing a pin and, for the first time in weeks, was all smiles and good will as he greeted his guests. He announced complete amnesty, restoring all confiscated lockers — even for Cindy Schwartz.

Sheldon was on cloud nine, lecturing at length on how things tended to fall into place. Feldstein was an enormously influential member of the Don't Care community, and his show of support was the completing brick in the superstructure of Mike's power base. With regard to Mike Otis, Don't Care High cared one-hundred percent.

By the next week, however, Sheldon felt the need to move ahead. "It's time for a confrontation," he announced to Paul one day over ginger ale and stale cake at Sheldon's house. "It's time to have a mammoth rally."

Paul choked. "What happened to polite and restrained? What happened to not breaking any rules?"

"We still won't break any rules. I envision everyone assembling in front of the school at about seven-thirty in the morning, and greeting all the staff members with our solidarity." He cleared his throat. "And it might not hurt to tip off a few members of the local press to come by and cover it."

"In this city?" said Paul dubiously. "They'd never show up."

"Sure they will. We're Don't Care High. We killed the science fair and trashed Laguna. They won't know we plan to be peaceful. And our numbers are good. I expect almost everybody to turn out to support Mike."

And so the word went out. The entire student body was expected at seven-thirty Friday morning to take its big stand. The spreading of the news was a very serious business, and Sheldon and Paul took no chances with the publicity.

"It's better to have every student hear this a million times than risk having one guy forget to show up," Sheldon declared to the LaPaz triplets as he recruited them as P.R. representatives.

The LaPazes, with their triple action, combed the school, leaving no stone unturned in their search for students who had not yet heard of Friday's planned events. Feldstein, who was a great observer of the passing parade, reported that enthusiasm was running high, and that he'd yet to come across anyone who did not plan to attend. Sheldon and Paul did a great deal of mingling personally, just to make sure. Sheldon impressed upon the students that all their weeks of support would be for nothing if Friday did not go well.

This added an air of tension to the school. The students bore down as all the minute details of the rally were worked out. Car pools were arranged, and large groups of students formed wake-up call pacts, as no one wanted to oversleep and let Mike down. Peter Eversleigh arranged to cancel his dental appointment, and Phil Gonzalez stayed home while his parents went out of town because they insisted on leaving a day early. On Friday, the sum total of everyone's devotion and dedication to Mike Otis would be packed into an hour and a half, and there did not exist a reason good enough for missing it.

On Thursday, excitement was running high as plans moved into the home stretch. The three final briefing sessions were held during the three lunch hours to cover the entire student body, and Sheldon resumed his old position atop an end table. Sheldon was a natural leader, Paul reflected, as his friend stirred up the crowd over the importance of tomorrow. When Sheldon took over the organization of things, Paul would easily be swept up and would follow him blindly. And under such circumstances, there would always be a last-minute twist that Sheldon would throw into the pot without consulting anyone. Paul knew that it had happened again when Sheldon announced that tomorrow morning everyone would try to dress exactly like Mike.

"Like *Mike*?" Paul repeated as a hum of surprise went up from the third period lunch crowd.

Sheldon reached into a large art portfolio and pulled out a set of enormous flash cards.

"*One*," he announced, holding up the first illustrated card. "The hair. Slick. Greased back. *Two*" — Sheldon moved on to the second card — "The raincoat. Big. Dirty beige preferably, but any dull color will do. *Three*. The shirt. Bright colors. Pink and fluorescent green are best. Remember, Mike never wears patterns or plaids. *Four*. . . ."

Paul watched as Sheldon continued through the long, turned-up jeans with the safety pins, and the black dress shoes. Then he began to run the group through it again and again, holding up the illustrated cards. By the end of the briefing, Sheldon merely had to shout out the number, and the students would give the appropriate response in one great unified voice.

"*Six!*"

"The shoes!" chanted the crowd. "Black! Dress! No high heels or alligator!"

"You've got it!" called Sheldon. "And tomorrow morning I want to see it!"

Sheldon did not even wait for Paul's protest before offering his explanation. "Dressing like Mike is something I thought up lying in bed last night. It'll give the rally a visual aspect for the TV cameras."

"Have you called those guys yet?" asked Paul nervously.

"Not yet. We'll have to get together on what we're going to say. Later, though. Fourth period lunch is starting to come in for briefing."

"Another episode of 'How to Look like a Weird-o in Six Easy Steps,'" said Paul sarcastically.

Sheldon laughed. "Don't worry. Everything's going to be great."

Morale among the teaching staff was approaching the breaking point. On Thursday after classes, a delegation of teachers, headed by the semiambulatory Mr. Willis, filed into Mr. Gamble's office to make its plea for sanity.

"Look, Henry," said Mr. Willis reasonably, "we agree with you that this Mike Otis thing is a farce. But we're the ones who have to put up with it in the classrooms hour after hour, day after day. We've been taking it for a long time, but now you've got to give us a break. All this has to stop, and if that means making Otis president again, then so be it."

Mr. Gamble leaned forward. "You know my opinion on the subject, and the answer is no."

"But Henry!" wailed Miss Vlorque. "You don't have to sit through seven polite, reasonable speeches every day! You don't have to listen to seven rounds of applause! You don't have to watch the morning sun glint off thirty safety pins! It's like teaching tinsel! And then when the class is over and you can finally escape from your thirty safety pins, the halls are teeming with them! Safety pins! Everywhere! There's nowhere to hide! You can't escape them. . . ." Her voice trailed off.

"As you can see," said Mr. Hennessey, "it's affecting us all in different ways. Willis gets aggravated, Vlorque lets it push her towards a nervous breakdown, I just get mad. When they start giving me all that sincere garbage, I lose my patience. But the common denominator, Henry, is that it's driving us all nuts."

"And did you hear the sounds coming from the cafeteria today?" added Mrs. Wolfe. "They're working up some kind of ritual chant!"

Miss Vlorque emitted a quick, nervous giggle. "They'll probably start doing it in class! I don't know if I can face it!"

"Just let them try it in *my* class!" thundered Mr. Hennessey. "I'll — "

"Calm down, everybody," ordered the vice-principal sharply. "I hear you all, and I realize it's a problem. I figured this would all die out when we asked for new nominations. Maybe I was wrong." He turned momentarily red. "I just can't stand the idea of some miserable upstart out there, who's responsible for the whole thing, laughing at us when we have to give in!"

"Look, Henry," said Mr. Willis, "if it was the principle of the thing that concerned us, we'd be on your side one-hundred percent. But it's just not that important. The kids aren't breaking any rules, and we're fighting for our sanity. Now, we've talked to the boss, and he says he'll go along with whatever we decide, so long as he gets to make the announcement. So what do you say?"

Mr. Gamble slumped back in his chair. "All right, they can have Otis — they can have anything! I'll have it announced tomorrow."

When he returned home from school that afternoon, Paul met his mother rushing through the lobby of the building.

"Oh, Paul — here you are! Thank goodness!"

"You're going to Auntie Nancy's house," said Paul wearily.

"Oh, the most terrible thing has happened! Your Uncle Harry was coming home from work early because he had a cold, and just as he was driving under a bridge, a cement block fell right through his windshield!"

"Was he hurt?" asked Paul anxiously.

"No, thank heaven, but when the window shattered in front of him, he thought he'd been shot! And it was on the *highway*! You know that highway always upsets me! I've got to get over there right away! Poor Nancy!"

"Poor Nancy? She's all right! No one dropped anything on her!"

"Yes, but it's always the wife who has to cope with these things. Remember when Dad broke his nose?

Oh, how I suffered! Anyway, there's no dinner. Perhaps you can get together with your friend Sheridan. If not, there's lots of cold meat for sandwiches. Oh, yes. There's a letter for you. Why are international car experts writing to you?"

"It's a long story, Mom," muttered Paul. "Don't worry. I'll be all right."

His mother rushed off, and Paul hurried into the elevator. He let himself into the apartment and snatched his letter off the hall table. It was postmarked Bern, Switzerland, from the International Automobile Collectors' Association. Intrigued, he opened it.

Dear Mr. Abrams,

We have examined the photographs you submitted, and we are unable to identify this car. We do not believe that it was produced by any auto manufacturer we know of, assuming any company would plead guilty to having turned out such a monstrous product.

Theoretically, this car does not exist. We are then presented with two conclusions as to what the car really is: 1) it is an elaborate, homemade production built quite literally from scratch; or 2) it is some kind of sculpture built by you for the purpose of baffling experts such as ourselves. This second theory is the favorite around here, and we would like you to know that we do not appreciate the gesture. However, on the off chance that this really is a functional automobile, please send some verification of this and we will be prepared to make you an offer for its purchase.

In an instant, the entire Mike Otis saga flashed before Paul's eyes: a bizarre figure at the end of the hallway; the nomination; the car; the confidential file; Finch, Oklahoma; the operator saying the number was disconnected; 106 Gordon Street; and the crowning glory — that wholesome family that raised more doubts than it answered.

Tomorrow twenty-six hundred people were going to get together at seven-thirty in the morning, dressed like complete idiots, to demonstrate on behalf of a man who no one understood beyond the fact that his only detectable desire was to be left alone. It was too much.

Suddenly Paul had his coat on and was out the door, down the elevator, and threading his way through the garbage-laden streets like a man possessed. This was it. Showdown. Maybe Sheldon had no qualms about organizing great crusades on behalf of the mystery man, but Paul Abrams could bear it no longer. He refused to live one more hour without a solution to the puzzle that was Mike Otis. And there was only one way to get it.

His jaw squared with determination, he marched the fifteen blocks to Mike's apartment building, burst into the lobby, and paused in front of the doorman. Yes, he had every right in the world to be there, he told himself. Swiss auto experts were interested in buying Mike's car, and he owed it to

Mike to tell him about it. Then he would maneuver the conversation around to include Mike's ersatz home town, address, and phone number. It would all work in very naturally. When he left this place, by God, he would have it all!

"Otis, 7E," he told the doorman confidently. "My name's Paul Abrams. I'm a friend of Mike's from school."

The man phoned upstairs, and Paul was surprised at how quickly he was admitted. He hadn't been entirely sure how Mike would respond to a visitor at his home. When he got to the apartment, he found out why. It had been Mrs. Otis, not Mike, who had invited him up so readily.

"Michael's out on an errand now, but I expect him back any minute. Please come in and sit down."

Paul allowed himself to be seated in front of a glass of milk and a few cookies while Mike's mother made small talk. His head was spinning. Perching on a fire escape watching the Otises was nothing compared to the jolt of actually speaking with a member of this incredibly normal family.

"Mr. Otis and I have often wondered about this Don Carey High School. It seems like such a . . . strange place. We've never received so much as a letter or a telephone call from them."

True, thought Paul, but even if there were a notice, it would end up in the dead letter office via 106 Gordon Street. Aloud, he said, "Oh, it's not strange, Mrs. Otis. They just . . . uh . . . don't want to interfere with individual development."

"Well, we were just afraid that Michael might be left out of things."

"I can safely say," said Paul devoutly, "that Mike is never left out of anything." He looked up as the front door opened and Mike entered, carrying a bag of groceries.

Because of the positioning of the door frame, the first thing Mike saw was Paul, sitting at the kitchen table. In perplexity, he checked the number on the front door. Yes, this was his apartment, all right.

"Oh good, dear, you're back. Paul is here."

Cautiously, Mike entered the kitchen and put his parcel down on the counter, but the beady eyes never left Paul.

"Hi, Mike."

"Hi." Mike looked at his mother plaintively, as if to say "How did this happen?"

Mrs. Otis refilled the cookie plate and poured a glass of water for her son. "Well, I must go and finish my ironing. I'll leave you two boys to chat."

The conversation didn't start. Intimidated by the situation of facing Mike in his own home, Paul completely forgot about his Swiss car experts, and just sat, looking uncomfortably at the student body ex-president. Mike looked back, his system on a sort of bland red alert. This confrontation reeked of the things at school that he didn't understand — right here on his own turf.

Finally, Paul blurted, "There is no Finch, Oklahoma, is there, Mike?"

The beady eyes grew even more veiled than usual. After a pause, Mike said, "Probably not."

"There's no such thing as apartment eleven twenty-five at one-oh-six Gordon Street, either, and the phone number in your file is disconnected, right?" Mike made no reply, so Paul continued. "Why does the school have all this phony information about you?"

Mike looked all around the kitchen and then paused before replying. "I had to put something on the registration forms."

"So *you* gave them all that! On purpose!"

"Nobody said it had to be right."

"But why?" Paul insisted. "Why can't people know where you come from and where you live and what your telephone number is?"

Paul could almost see the wheels turning in Mike's head. His answer, when it came, was, "I like it better this way." Then he shrugged very slightly, but together with his words, it seemed to say everything about the man Sheldon had picked to be president.

Suddenly, Paul felt very foolish, trudging all over town, interrupting people's lives to solve the Mike Otis puzzle. There was no puzzle. It was just Mike's nature, the fact that Mike liked it better that way. The mysterious Mike Otis was just a guy — an offbeat, bizarre, crazy, weird guy, but just a guy nonetheless.

Paul stood up, his mind at ease, or at least as much at ease as it could be, considering he was scheduled to participate in a twenty-six hundred man rally in the morning. Should he mention it to Mike? No. Better leave well enough alone. "Well, Mike, I'm going to take off now. See you at school tomorrow."

Mrs. Otis breezed into the kitchen. "Michael will drive you home, Paul."

Mike looked pained.

"Oh, that's okay," said Paul. "I don't live too far."

"It's raining and you don't have an umbrella," she insisted. "Off you go, now."

The black behemoth rode quite comfortably, and on the way home, Paul remembered his original excuse for visiting Mike that day. He told Mike about the letter from Switzerland and the interest shown by the International Automobile Collectors' Association in purchasing the mystery car.

Mike seemed unimpressed. "I like it," he said, indicating the car was not for sale.

Paul looked at Mike in sudden admiration. "You made this, didn't you? You built this car totally from scratch!"

Mike made no reply, and at first Paul thought there was to be no answer. And quite a few seconds had gone by before Mike said,

"Sometimes I have a lot of spare time."

So the mystery of the car was solved, too. It was the closest thing to a straight yes anyone would ever get out of Mike. Paul shook his head. "Mike, do you have any idea how great an achievement it is to make a working car out of *nothing*?"

Mike pulled over to the curb in front of Paul's building. "Probably not."

Over the phone, Sheldon told Paul that he had already alerted the media himself about tomorrow's rally. The fact that he had not waited for Paul to do it undoubtedly meant that he had exaggerated grotesquely. Tomorrow the school would be crawling with reporters, all expecting a bloodbath. Paul decided not to tell Sheldon about his unscheduled trip to the Otises'. Not knowing the real truth about Mike had never bothered Sheldon anyway. Maybe in a few months, if Sheldon brought it up. . . .

"And now it's time for City Update!" exclaimed Flash Flood. "Today's reminder: Avoid inhaling, because the garbage strike shows no signs of ending! Be prepared for the worst, because that's what we always get in the greatest city in the world!"

As he got ready for bed, Paul was aware of a few butterflies in his stomach over tomorrow. He felt better about Mike than ever before, but organized student protests made him very nervous. When the teachers arrived at school to find twenty-six hundred demonstrators dressed like Mike, they were going to freak out.

Before calling it a night, Paul made a point of checking on the building across the street. Rabbit Man was still nowhere to be found, and the fire-eater didn't seem to be in, either. The big football fan was crouched in front of his TV set watching a game. There was a new enigma on that floor, however. Three windows over from the end zone was a whole apartment lit at least six or seven times as brightly as anything else in sight. In the living room sat a man, a woman, and two children, all wearing sunglasses. Whenever they moved, great shadows were cast in all directions. Even with the lights out and the blinds drawn, Paul's room was still partly illuminated from the Fifty-Thousand-Watt Family across the way.

The people next door had moved out, taking Steve with them. Somewhere he was waging his continual TV battle against the forces of evil, and piling up medals and leading ladies like cordwood. A group of young intellectuals now lived there. They borrowed sugar a lot, and spent the rest of every day arguing philosophy. If it hadn't been for their discussion, Paul might never have gotten to sleep that night.

13

The next day, Paul was up before dawn to begin the task of converting himself into a Mike Otis look-alike. He moved about the apartment on tiptoe for fear of waking up his parents, as he was not keen on explaining his behavior and that of his twenty-six hundred-odd fellow students. Feeling more than a little ridiculous, he shuffled into the bathroom, repeating Sheldon's chant under his breath.

"*One*. The hair. Slick. Greased back." From the medicine cabinet he produced a tube of hair cream, squeezed a minor mountain of it into his palm, and began plastering his light brown curls to his scalp.

He reflected glumly that he would obviously be the only one fool enough to get himself up this way, except for Mike himself, and maybe Sheldon. No one would even show up. It was going to be a horrible bust.

For the shirt, he selected the blood-red monstrosity given to him by Auntie Nancy for his birthday. He had never dreamed that he would wear it anywhere but to Edmondo's. Then came the jeans, which he rolled up at the cuffs and tacked down with two bright silver safety pins. The raincoat and shoes were his father's, both several sizes too large, but essential to the overall effect.

Then came a decision. Should he make his escape while the coast was clear? Or should he risk a bowl of cereal, since he was dying of starvation. And so it was for the sake of a bowl of corn flakes that Paul's escape was foiled when his mother appeared in the kitchen.

"Paul, what are you doing up? It's only six-fifteen. You're far too early for — " She rubbed her eyes, opened them, and screamed in shock.

Within seconds, Paul's father was on the scene. "What happened?" Disoriented without his glasses, he squinted at the figure sitting at the table. "Who's that?"

"That's your son!"

"No, it isn't. Where's his hair?"

"It's me, Dad," said Paul in agitation. "I'm going to school early today."

"Why do you look like that?"

Paul turned red. "Well . . . it's just something

we've got going at school. I'm . . . uh . . . meeting some people there this morning, and this is the way we're dressing."

Mr. Abrams leaned forward to get a closer look at his son. "What is it — Weasel Day?"

Paul smiled weakly. "Something like that."

Mrs. Abrams folded her arms. "I don't care what it is! You're not leaving the house looking this way!"

"I have to go, Mom," Paul argued. "The whole school's going to be there. We're supporting the student body president."

"Aha!" cried his mother. "This is the work of that awful Mike Otis!"

"Exactly what *is* going on this morning?" Mr. Abrams asked.

"It's really tough to explain, Dad," said Paul earnestly. "Couldn't I tell you about it some other time? I've got to get going."

"Not until you wash your hair and change your clothes!" cried his mother.

"Oh, just let him be," said his father soothingly. "This kind of thing always happens in big city schools. It means Paul's fitting in. Don't forget — we're not in the boonies anymore."

"But Cyril — "

Paul headed for the door. "I'll be back about four, Mom. Bye, Dad."

He usually walked to school, but today he decided to take the subway, sticking to the darker areas. He met Sheldon on the platform, and the two indulged in some good-natured laughter at each other's appearance.

"Let's face it, Shel, it looks okay on Mike, but on us . . . ."

Sheldon adjusted his enormous gray raincoat. "I know what you're saying. Let's just hope that our troops remember to get up for the war, because I don't want to look like this alone." He took a deep breath. "All right. Let's move out."

Perhaps the worst experience of Mr. Gamble's life was his arrival at school that morning. Though he had been briefed on the incidents at both the science fair and Laguna, he had never actually witnessed Don't Care High in mass congregation, and when he drove along 22nd Street, the sight that met his eyes was Sheldon's greatest turnout yet — for all intents and purposes the entire population of Don Carey High School: twenty-six hundred replicas of Mike Otis.

The entire front courtyard of the school was packed tightly with students, who stood in an orderly fashion listening to another Otis clone bellowing out a speech from the front steps. Over the crowd waved a huge cloth banner, attached to two mobile poles. It read: WE WANT MIKE BACK. Stuck through it was a five-foot-long silver safety pin. To make matters worse, there were quite a few spectators stopped on the sidewalk to watch the goings-on, and — yes! television cameras!

In a rage, the vice-principal wheeled onto the driveway and gunned the engine for the parking lot, then slammed on the brakes, stopping in a squeal of tires behind another stopped vehicle which blocked the narrow lane. It was Mr. Morrison parked ahead. His head protruded from the window, and he was watching the proceedings with a look of intense bliss. Impatiently, Mr. Gamble leaned on the horn.

Mr. Morrison looked back at him and called, "I believe in these kids, Henry!"

"You're in the way! Move along!"

Both cars drove into the lot and parked side by side.

The two men found the rest of the staff assembled in the teachers' lounge, where the atmosphere was electric.

Mr. Hennessey was issuing rapid-fire threats while unconsciously dismembering the Yellow Pages; Mr. Willis, who had bravely abandoned his crutches, was limping a constant figure-eight in the center of the room; Mrs. Carling knelt on a small coffee table and peered furtively out through the curtains, shaking her head and saying, "Son-of-a-gun. Son-of-a-gun. Son-of-a-*gun*!" Try as he might, Mr. Morrison could not wipe the grin off his face.

Wordlessly, Mr. Gamble looked out the window at his unrecognizable student body. Then he turned to his beaten staff. Shaking his head in disbelief, he started down the hall for the school's front door.

At the rally, Sheldon was in his glory. The day was shaping up into an enormous success with a near perfect turnout. Slim Kroy was playing a rousing rendition of his now-legendary *Mike Otis Tuba Solo*, by popular demand, when Mr. Gamble appeared on the front stairs. The vice-principal held up his hands for silence and the crowd grew still, but the two hundred fifty-pound Slim kept on playing.

"Stop that!" snapped Mr. Gamble irritably, and Slim hastily ended his serenade. "One more oom-pah out of you, and you will be suspended! Now, where's Otis?"

This was the one question Sheldon was not prepared for. "He's . . . uh . . . somewhere. I mean . . . else. Somewhere else."

Mr. Gamble swallowed hard. "I'm not surprised. Well, when he shows up, tell him he's president."

"You *mean* it?" blurted Paul.

"I said it, didn't I? But just remember that this is a school, and despite any blessed events, we were kind of hoping to hold classes today. So break this nonsense up and have everyone in homeroom by nine." He spun on his heel and disappeared into the building.

Sheldon addressed the multitude. "We've just been informed that Mike Otis is now reinstated as student body president!" He started to say something else, but was completely drowned out as a colossal roar of pure, unadulterated joy erupted from the students. All at once, several hundred raincoats were spontaneously thrown into the air, and seemed to hang there for a moment, forming a canopy over unrestrained rejoicing and revelry. There were handshakes and backslaps and victory signs, and even an amount of hugging and kissing. Some students formed a snake-dance; others a conga line. Wayne-o ran around in circles, punching his fist into the air and yelling, "*Yeah!*" Rosalie

Gladstone actually took her gum out of her mouth and sat down on the ground so she could savor the moment. A group of boys led by Phil Gonzalez broke into a chant of "Mike! Mike! Mike!" Phil himself was yelling so loud that his face was scarlet and his eyes were tightly shut. Students were meeting in joyful embrace, congratulating each other, and then running on to other friends. Old grudges suddenly disintegrated as students were united under the banner of Mike Otis. In one particularly touching episode, Feldstein ran up and awarded a hearty handshake to his old enemy, Slim Kroy, who had discarded his tuba to join the festivities. It was the first time in years they had been seen together, and the students formed a circle around them to cheer the reconciliation. The two posed for a few pictures, with Feldstein straining to get his arm around Slim's enormous shoulders. Even Daphne Sylvester cheered. Paul noticed that the divine Daphne still looked remarkably gorgeous, exquisite, and dainty dressed like Mike Otis. Her greased-back hair only emphasized her fine-boned face, and even her massive raincoat could not hide her figure.

Once again, Sheldon's voice boomed over the scene. "Look, everybody! It's *Mike!* Our president is coming!"

Paul's eyes turned to the road. The black behemoth was making its way to the Don't Care parking lot, the man of the hour at the wheel. The crowd roared again, and several hundred students started off on a stampede for the driveway.

The moment was intense. Paul could see

Sheldon's face glowing bright red with pride as he watched his president make the turn into the school. Dick Oliver and Samuel Wiscombe stood like sentries at attention, rigidly holding up the poles that supported the banner. Ten feet into the driveway, Mike's car was mobbed by jubilant students shouting and banging on the windows. Hundreds more ran to join the welcoming committee, and the scene fairly exploded.

And suddenly it became too much for a boy from Saskatoon to handle. Paul felt he had to do something — anything — and, fueled by a rush of emotion, he made a running leap for the gleaming five-foot safety pin that pierced the WE WANT MIKE BACK banner.

His hands locked on the bottom metal bar, and he swung dangerously for an instant as the shocked Samuel and Dick struggled to keep the poles upright. Then his weight proved too much for the banner, and the cloth began to give way at the center of the sign. Paul held on for dear life to the pin, which swung like a pendulum as the cloth of the banner ripped right down the middle. He crashed to the ground and lay there, still holding the pin, which was attached to a long, thin strip of cloth, which was in turn trailing from what was left of the banner.

Two people were carried into the school that morning: Mike Otis on the shoulders of his deliriously happy supporters; and Paul Abrams, on his way to the nurse's office for repairs.

* * *

May I have your attention, please.
Here are the day's announcements.

Anyone who is interested in a lecture
on bird-watching can register after hours
today at the guidance office.

Oh, yes. Mike Otis is once again stu-
dent body president. You will recall that
he held this office once before and was
removed. No future date has been set for
his next impeachment, and so I don't
think I am premature in saying congrat-
ulations, Mike. That's all. Have a good
day.

A great roar of approval went up from the student
body.

Having soaked away his aches in the bathtub and
washed the grease out of his hair, Paul lay on his
bed in a predinner cooling-off period.

There was a tap at the door, and his mother
entered the room, all concern. "Paul, I've just been
on the phone with your Auntie Nancy. According to
her, you were on the evening news. What's all this
about you falling off a sign?"

"It wasn't a sign, Mom, it was a banner. And I
didn't fall. I swung to the ground on a safety pin."

She frowned in perplexity. "According to Nancy,
it was a student activist demonstration. That's not
the kind of thing your father and I want to see you
involved in."

"It wasn't activism; we were supporting our student body president — let me finish — who isn't a roughneck, or a gangster, or a bum, but who is a great guy."

"But Nancy said —"

"She wasn't there, Mom. You have to trust *me* for a change."

"I do, dear. But after that awful basketball game . . . and the way you were dressed this morning. It's all so bizarre. I'm afraid there are too many agitators at this school of yours."

Paul laughed out loud, but decided against telling her that there were exactly two agitators at Don't Care High, and she was looking at one of them. "You're talking as though I was throwing fire bombs at riot police today. It was a simple little . . . get-together, and I was one of twenty-six hundred people."

"Yes, but you were the only one who fell off a sign."

"I *swung* from a *banner*. Anyway, it's all over, the president got his job back, the teachers are happy, the students are happy, and everything's back to normal at Don't Care — I mean, Don Carey. You have absolutely nothing to worry about."

The Don Carey High School rally was surprisingly well-documented in the Sunday papers, much to the delight of Sheldon, who bought multiple copies of each edition, and invited Paul over to admire them. Paul was a little less pleased, as the photograph that seemed to capture each city editor's fancy was a shot of the celebrating students, with the rally's lone casualty swinging dangerously from the banner in the background.

"It looks like you're about to fall off that sign," observed Jodi.

"It was a banner," Paul explained patiently. "And I swung to the ground."

"Yeah, well, I don't know what you call it," said Sheldon, "but we were pretty worried about you, Ambition, lying there in a heap. You were lucky. I figured on at least a couple of broken ribs."

Paul flushed. "I wonder what Mike thought about it all."

"It was really hard to tell," said Sheldon. "He seemed sort of confused, but I doubt he even wanted to understand. You know him. It's all pretty heavy-duty for a mellow guy like Mike. I have a lot of admiration for him."

Jodi frowned. "I don't get it. If this Mike Otis is the president, how can he not understand?"

"It's a very long story," said Paul painfully. "I mean *long*. You really don't want to know. And anyway, it's all over. Right, Shel?"

Sheldon's eyes gleamed. "Who can tell?"

Paul glared at him resentfully. "That's not funny."

The boys abandoned Flash Flood in favor of some roller-skating in Central Park, one of the few areas of New York relatively unscathed by the garbage strike. They rolled around for a while, reliving the old days of *The Otis Report*, then took to a well-shaded bench to rest up.

Sheldon yawned. "Well, Ambition, how does it feel to have the whole city in the palm of your hand?"

Paul laughed. "Just because Mike's back in office

doesn't mean we have the city in our hands."

"Oh, I don't know about that," said Sheldon. "At the drop of a hat we can mobilize an army of twenty-six hundred to any cause we choose, just by saying that Mike supports it. Think of the power. All we have to say is that Mike doesn't like the subways, and within hours, all twenty-six hundred of them will be out there cementing up the entrances." He grinned diabolically. Then, noticing Paul's uneasy expression, added, "But naturally we'll use the power to further the forces of good. Mike's name will go down with Superman and Robin Hood and all those guys."

"Just what are these great plans of yours?" asked Paul warily.

"Well, I figure on helping out with some worthy causes. That way, good charitable work will get done, and at the same time we'll keep the school's profile high and punch up Mike's image. We'll need about one of those per month. Then we'll get Mike to support all the sports teams, so we can expect trophies left, right, and center. And whenever something like the science fair comes along, we can pounce on it. But nothing will go wrong, because now we're so much smarter. And that's just for starters. We're a couple of creative guys. I'm sure that, as time goes by, we'll come up with even better ways to make use of Mike's great talents as a leader."

Paul sighed. "You know, Shel, Mike's been a real good sport about all this. Don't you think it's about time we just left him alone?"

"Are you kidding? I think Mike's just starting to get into it. Besides, aren't you interested in seeing how long it's going to take Daphne Sylvester to break down his defenses?"

"I don't know," mumbled Paul.

Sheldon fiddled with his skate laces. "Well, whether or not you agree with the long-range plan, remember the volleyball season is starting soon. And no one would like anything better than to see the Don Carey Sewer Men clean up this year," he chuckled, "in a manner of speaking."

Paul smiled grudgingly. "Well, I guess we could use Mike's power for the volleyball team."

"I knew you'd see it my way, Ambition. And then there's boys' basketball and baseball in the spring — this is just the beginning."

Paul had the apartment to himself that evening because his father was out of town and his mother was still on an extended lunch with Auntie Nancy. He improvised a dinner which consisted largely of potato chips, with an emaciated chicken breast serving as the main course. He considered writing his Shakespeare paper, but dismissed that, knowing that Sheldon would write his the night before the deadline, and finishing early would leave Paul with nothing to do that night. So he switched on Stereo 99 to see what Flash Flood had to say.

There was a polite knock at the door, and Paul got up to answer it. He peered through the peephole and found himself staring through the distorted glass directly into the face of Mike Otis himself.

Paul opened the door. "Mike — what a surprise. Come on in." The student body president took three steps forward and stood in the hallway. He and Paul stared at each other for an awkward moment. Then Paul spoke again. "Do you want to sit down?"

"No thank you."

There was another uncomfortable moment, and then Paul realized that Mike didn't intend to say anything else without prompting.

"Well, is there anything I can do for you, Mike?"

"No."

"What I mean is . . . why did you come here?"

"There are a lot of things at this school I don't understand," Mike began. He paused. "But maybe you understand."

"And you've come for an explanation?" asked Paul with a sinking heart.

"No," said Mike. Another pause. "I seem to feel that someone might want to know this."

"What?"

"What I came here to say."

"Which is — ?"

"I'm moving."

Paul's heart skipped a beat. "Moving? When?"

"Pretty soon," said Mike. "I just wanted to tell you." And he fled the apartment just as abruptly as he had arrived.

Paul stood rooted to the floor, staring out the open door. He ran out into the hall, but Mike was gone. Then he made a headlong dash straight for the kitchen telephone.

14

The news stunned Don't Care High. On Monday, the word spread like wildfire, and the halls buzzed with shock. Mike Otis — president, sovereign, and charismatic hero — was leaving.

Right before classes, Sheldon and Paul descended on Mike and cross-examined him at length. Yes, it was true. Mike would be leaving on the weekend to relocate in the town of Astragal, Indiana. Friday would be his last day at school.

A quick trip to the library confirmed what Paul had immediately suspected — there was no town of Astragal in Indiana, nor in any other state, province, or country in the world. It was as real as

Finch, Oklahoma, and there was a certain logic in Mike's going there. Paul toyed with the idea of demanding to know Mike's real destination — uptown Manhattan? Europe? — but he decided against it. He owed Mike that much privacy.

Sheldon was devastated. "How can he do this to us? When you take on the responsibilities of office, you can't just run away! You have to stay on and serve!"

"He never took on any responsibilities," Paul pointed out. "We took them on for him."

"Don't bother me with technicalities! When Mike leaves, our whole empire will crumble! This is terrible!"

Wayne-o was so distressed by Mike's leaving that he took to punctuality, arriving at all classes exactly on time to keep his mind from wandering to subjects that only caused him pain. Peter Eversleigh dropped gum and went back whole-hog on licorice. Feldstein was devastated, abandoning his stairwell and sitting for long hours in front of 205C in a reportedly sulky mood. Sometimes Slim Kroy sat with him, cradling his silent tuba. The LaPaz triplets began bickering among themselves. And Daphne Sylvester went into deep mourning, which became her very well.

Phil Gonzalez wanted to build Mike a monument. "You know, like the pyramids. Mike's at least as important as those old pharaoh guys."

The WOW Connection would have settled for changing the name of the school to Mike Otis High. Cindy Schwartz was holding out for seven days of skywriting and fireworks. Trudy Helfield wanted to petition the mayor to close off city streets and have a parade. Slim Kroy would accept nothing less than the minting of a commemorative coin. All these ideas were dismissed as rather extravagant.

"Well, if we can't do any of that stuff," said Wayne-o, "we may as well have a party."

Sheldon pounced on the idea. "Yes, and despite his greatness, it's fitting that we should send him off as a normal Don't Care student, because that's what he'll want to be remembered as."

So the next morning, Sheldon and Paul appeared in the guidance office to appeal to Mr. Morrison for help.

Mr. Morrison sighed. "It's a wonderful idea, boys, but I really don't think the school has the money. I can try, but I'm sure the answer will be no."

"What about the raffle money?" blurted Paul.

Mr. Morrison grimaced. "We've only sold eleven tickets, and *I* sold all of those. I'm afraid I'm going to have to cancel the raffle."

"Well, how many tickets are there?" asked Paul.

"Five thousand."

"All right, Mr. Morrison," said Sheldon evenly, "if we can sell your five thousand and then ten thousand more on top of that by three-thirty on Thursday, can we have that party on Friday night?"

Mr. Morrison was aghast. "Why . . . of course. But how will you — I mean, how?"

"This is the Mike Otis Raffle," said Sheldon with grim determination. "And if we can't get rid of those tickets, we don't deserve to have had him as our president."

Once again Sheldon's strident voice rang out in

the cafeteria over the three lunch periods. "So sell those raffle tickets, and on Friday night, we'll give Mike the send-off he deserves!" The students cheered with enthusiasm.

Mr. Morrison could hardly believe his good fortune. As soon as the word was out, the guidance office was mobbed with would-be sellers of raffle tickets. By one o'clock, he was faced with the inconceivable situation of turning away eager students because he was out of ticket books. By two o'clock, his emergency rush order for ten thousand more tickets arrived at his office, to be snapped up even quicker than their predecessors. By three o'clock, they were gone again and, in his ecstasy, Mr. Morrison ordered another five thousand and tripled the prize, promising two more color television sets.

"What are you going to do," snarled Mr. Gamble, "when these idiots come back to tell you they forgot to sell the tickets, and you're stuck with three TV's?"

The old Mr. Morrison would have been intimidated, but the new one was in a light, bubbly mood from the school spirit he knew was behind him. "Well — ha, ha — there are three major networks. I can watch them all at the same time."

That, however, was going to be unnecessary. The next morning, the money started pouring in. All day the guidance office and surrounding halls were full of students handing in ticket stubs and cash. As each student submitted his gains, he picked up new tickets to sell, until the whole twenty thousand were in circulation. At one dollar a ticket, the school stood to make a fortune. It was the ultimate raffle, Mr. Morrison decided, his cup running over. That monster called "lack of interest," his archenemy and longtime tormentor, now lay at his feet, beaten into submission.

Paul himself managed to unload three books of tickets in his apartment building, and Sheldon got rid of a like amount in and around his home and at a boarding pass soiree of his father's. The most successful seller by a wide margin was Feldstein at seventeen books. But even the most reluctant student made an effort to combine with a few friends on one or two books. When the selling binge reached its official close by three-thirty on Thursday, not a single unsold ticket was returned, and Mr. Morrison confirmed a total of $20,000.

Sheldon went in as student negotiator, and extorted enough money from the guidance counselor for the party of everyone's dreams. Almost as an afterthought, he and Paul went and convinced Mike that his attendance Friday night was mandatory. Mike, who was already vaguely aware of the raffle and its possible relation to him, agreed to be there. It was, after all, in his honor, and was probably somehow connected to his immense popularity.

Paul returned home from school that afternoon emotionally exhausted from the excitement of the week, and somewhat disheartened by the news that Sheldon had arranged for tomorrow night's party to be catered by the pizza parlor that specialized in the tomato sauce patented under the name *Rocco*. Sheldon had planned the party with his usual sense of the dramatic, and had rented a sound system so powerful that Paul wasn't sure the

224

decaying gymnasium building could stay standing around it.

When he got home, Paul was greeted by his mother with the news flash of the century. After years of negotiation, Auntie Nancy was getting her dishwasher. He tried to sound enthusiastic about it. He had never been a major fan of Auntie Nancy, and had been secretly pulling for a few more years of stand-off. Mrs. Abrams sensed this, so she waited for her husband, breaking the wonderful news to him as he stepped over the threshold.

But her husband was in a towering rage. "I can't believe it! I've never heard of anything so stupid in my life! I stopped by the License Bureau to book your driving test, Paul, and you'll never *believe* what they told me! No one under eighteen years old is allowed to drive in New York City!"

"You mean we've been breaking the law?" asked Paul.

"Everywhere else in the world has it one way! *Here* they have to be different! I've been chewing nails all afternoon!"

"I guess that means no more driving," said Paul, who was just getting to like the idea of being a Manhattan motorist.

"Are you kidding?" his father howled. "They're not stopping me — and you, of course. We'll drive on Long Island! We'll drive in Yonkers! We'll drive in Jersey! We'll drive in Connecticut. . . ."

As Mr. Abrams continued to list all the places where they would go to drive, Paul couldn't help laughing over this latest development in his personal relationship with the automobile. In Saskatoon, he'd been dying to drive; in New York, he'd lost interest. He'd been scared of it, and had triumphed over that. And now he liked it, but was no longer allowed to do it. There was a message in there somewhere.

The staff of Don't Care High was in extremely good spirits that week. Most of the teachers were quite happy at the thought of seeing the last of Mike Otis, and Paul, despite his dedication to the president, could not honestly blame them. Most had had nothing against the old Don't Care High, and were hoping to see a return to normalcy.

> *May I have your attention, please. Here are the day's announcements.*
> *Student body president Mike Otis, as of this weekend, will no longer be with us. There will be a farewell party tonight at eight o'clock for Mike. While no one enjoys a good party more than I do, loss of life is not necessary for a good time. Also bear in mind that the money that would be used to repair our gymnasium, should it be destroyed this evening, has already been spent on other destroyed gymnasia, so please be careful.*
> *That's all. Have a good day, and good luck, Mike.*

Mr. Gamble was all smiles, and had readily consented to the party in light of the lasting peace which would follow it. He thought of the magic moment when he'd first heard the news that Mike was leaving; he could still hear Mrs. Carling's "Son-of-a-gun" which had brought him out to investigate.

Mr. Willis was particularly pleased because, in addition to Mike's departure, other things in his life were right back on the track. His ankle was healed, his print dryer was replaced by a nice modern new one, his office was rebuilt, and his classes were starting to produce some pretty good work — even the last period group. He also knew that the honor would be his to preside over Mike's final class at Don Carey High School. He had prepared several juicy comments for the occasion. Mr. Willis would never see this final class, however. Friday would be the day that the many bags of uncollected garbage sitting outside in front of his house would spontaneously combust, threatening the whole block. He would spend the day dealing with the police and fire departments and the insurance company. So Mike's last scheduled class was never convened.

Sheldon and Paul both skipped dinner and stayed at school to help set up the equipment and decorations for the party. They watched as the three-pronged decorating committee, headed by the LaPazes, worked to transform the broken-down Don't Care gymnasium into an opulent banquet hall or, at the very least, a reasonable facsimile thereof. Sheldon personally supervised the installation of the massive twelve-by-fifteen-foot Mike Otis poster, which was an enlargement of the eight-by-ten glossy portrait. This he ordered placed behind the makeshift stage from which he intended to conduct the evening's brief ceremonies. Directly to the right of this was the d.j.'s station, from which the d.j. could control the sound system and the many lights which were strategically placed around the gym.

By seven o'clock, the room was festooned with colored streamers, balloons, and hundreds of handmade tinfoil safety pins. The enormous banner, FAREWELL MIKE, was hung over the stage by the WOW Connection, and Samuel pierced it with the five-foot safety pin, saying to Paul,

"How about you don't fall off this one, okay?"

Feldstein had scored a deal on three thousand rhinestone-studded safety pins, and these were delivered shortly after seven to be handed out at the door as souvenirs. All was in readiness when, a little past seven-thirty, the first of the students began to arrive.

Mr. Gamble was there, heading up a security force which consisted of Mr. Hennessey, Mr. Schmidt, Coach Murphy, and a few others. Mr. Morrison was supposed to be there, too, but, uncharacteristically, he was late.

Since Don Carey had never hosted an extracurricular activity in living memory, no one had anticipated the space problem. As eight o'clock came and went, the gym got more and more mobbed as well as hotter by degrees. And still students kept pouring in. Once again Don't Care High was humming, but this hum was more of a buzz, the sound of twenty-six hundred students supercharged with nervous anticipation.

At eight-fifteen, Feldstein made his entrance,

and the locker baron was indeed a splendid sight. He had trimmed back down to his normal weight and wore studded black jeans and even blacker glossy boots. His black leather jacket was zipped down far enough to reveal a heavy sterling silver chain, from which hung a gleaming combination lock, his symbol of office, worn only on official occasions.

Five minutes later, Wayne-o breezed in, and his appearance was no less impressive. He was immaculate as a bridegroom in a three-piece charcoal gray business suit with silk tie and alligator shoes. His face was scrubbed and shining, and his hair was in perfect order, parted so crisply that it looked as though an ax had been used rather than a brush and comb.

The call went up in the gym: "Hey, check out Wayne-o!" but Paul only had eyes for Daphne Sylvester. She was wrapped in a silver minidress, and it looked as though the style of what she wore had been designed exclusively with her in mind. She had put her hair up, and a few charming curls framed her perfect face. She was a vision.

Wayne-o was the last of the invited student body, and the crowd, shoulder to shoulder in the packed gymnasium, awaited only one more addition — the guest of honor.

Finally, at twenty-five minutes to nine, the epitome of fashionable lateness, Mike appeared in the doorway, looking exactly as he always looked, adding only a loosely-knotted, narrow, leopard-skin tie to his attire.

A roar of excitement went up in the gym, and

Mike was forced to shake endless hands and receive numerous slaps on the back as Sheldon and Paul escorted him through the sea of well-wishers to the stage area. Slim Kroy fumbled with his tuba in the crush, and blared out the *Mike Otis Tuba Solo* as the student body president stood with Sheldon and Paul before the adoring crowd. The cheering and applause went on for a few more minutes, and then silence fell, for it was time for the ceremonies to begin.

Sheldon stepped up to the microphone. "Students of Don't Care High, we stand together on the threshold of great sadness, yet there is also great happiness in our gathering, because. . . ."

It was a magnificent speech, Paul reflected, full of bittersweet emotion, and delivered in Sheldon's inimitable style. He spoke of feelings Mike had supposedly shared, and comments Mike had allegedly made. He spoke of Mike's deep sense of pride in the school's progress, and told how Mike expected them to carry on even in his absence. Paul marveled at how Sheldon had the nerve to say these things with Mike standing right beside him. He looked from Mike's empty countenance to the twenty-six hundred shining, attentive faces in the audience, and finally to the disgust and suppressed hostility mirrored by Mr. Gamble.

". . . and so it's true that we're losing a president, but we have gained as well, in terms of the better person I am, you are, we all are for having known Mike Otis!"

There was thunderous applause, and then Paul pushed Mike up in front of the microphone. Dead silence reigned as all waited with bated breath. Mike looked at Paul plaintively, but Paul responded with a confident nod and motioned for Mike to begin.

Mike opened his speech with an agonizingly long pause, which had everyone straining in intense concentration. Then he said, "There are a lot of things at this school I don't understand."

The gym went wild in appreciation of this tension-breaking, witty comment.

"I didn't do anything," Mike continued.

This was the president's famous modesty, and it met with great applause.

"Thanks for inviting me to the party. Bye."

Sheldon ran up to Mike, raised his arms in the air in victory, and shouted, "Bring on the food! *Let the music begin!*"

What followed was a wild blur of floor-shaking music, gyrating bodies, and the tomato sauce patented under the name *Rocco*. No sooner had the music started than Daphne Sylvester grabbed Mike by the scruff of the neck and hauled him bodily out onto the dance floor. Hundreds of students followed suit, hundreds mobbed the pizza tables, and still hundreds more formed into groups and discussed Mike's speech over the incredible din of the music.

Don't Care High got down. The students danced and celebrated furiously as all the pent-up frustration of Mike's departure found its release from them with the intensity of the firing of a retrorocket. For those students who had spent their whole high school careers at Don Carey, it was their first ever school dance, and for that one Friday night anyway, the Don't Care gymnasium was the hottest spot in the greatest city in the world. Everyone was dancing, and eating, and laughing, and shouting.

Daphne Sylvester still had hold of Mike, and it looked as though the entire WOW Connection was dancing with the LaPazes, but it was hard to tell on the spectacular strobe-lit dance floor. Sheldon was in the middle of it, too, dancing with everyone and no one at the same time, his arms flailing, his expression blissful. Feldstein was hanging out by the large poster. He would not dance, as he felt it was inconsistent with his dignity. Paul thought he saw Slim Kroy wrapping up extra pieces of pizza and hiding them in his tuba, but he couldn't be sure.

Even Peter Eversleigh danced for a couple of numbers, although he would have preferred to sit on the sidelines and assess the conceptuality of the situation. But Rosalie Gladstone seemed to have taken a permanent liking to him which, Paul thought with a smile, was Rosalie's problem.

Songs changed, and partners changed, and the night raged on, but the enthusiasm just seemed to grow. Sheldon was covered with glory, Phil Gonzalez was covered in sweat, and Wayne-o was covered in pizza, suit and all. At ten o'clock, Daphne was obliged to surrender Mike to the public, whereupon the entire female population of Don't Care High waited its turn to dance with the legend. Paul made desperate attempts to get near Daphne, but whenever he got up the nerve to ask her to dance, someone else was always there first. This went on for an hour and a half, after which Daphne reclaimed Mike, and the opportunity vanished just as quickly as it had appeared. In disgust, Paul tromped across the gym and sat down beside Peter Eversleigh, who was eating licorice and staring into the colored lights.

"I'm thinking of taking up stick, Peter. Can you stake me some?"

"No, dude, don't do that. She's too tall for you, anyway."

Paul jammed two complete sticks into his mouth and chewed violently. "I was hoping I'd grow."

Suddenly, a voice bellowed over the music: *"Have no fear! King Arthur is here!"* Mr. Morrison burst onto the scene. His hair was wild, his expression was ecstatic, his normally conservative clothes were disheveled, and his breath smelled suspiciously of beer.

Sheldon and Wayne-o rushed to his side. "Mr. Morrison, are you all right?"

"Sir Pryor! Sir Stitsky! Valiant warriors of Don't Care High — I mean, Don Carey — oh, what's the difference? Fear not, for all is well in the realm. Thanks to all you wonderful knights, I have slain the monster Lack of Interest and punched the villain in the nose!"

Sheldon and Wayne-o looked over at Mr. Gamble, but he was still standing.

"No, not that villain — my analyst — my *ex*-analyst! I hath smote him a blow. And that is when I sought out a pot of bonny ale to slake my thirst. So I am now King Arthur, which I can confirm, as I performed the coronation personally in the Cathedral

— just before they threw me out in a minor *coup d'etat*. But I assure you my throne is secure."

"Oh, Mr. Morrison!" groaned Wayne-o.

"That's 'Your Majesty,'" corrected the king. He leaned over to them and said in a whisper, "But confidentially, I think I may have drunk too much, because, while the throne is steady, this room seems to be wobbling quite a lot."

Sheldon signaled Paul and, with Wayne-o's help, the three of them tried to maneuver Mr. Morrison away from his fellow staff members. Meanwhile, the party had lost none of its momentum. The students were showing signs of the ability to carry on until noon when, at midnight, Mr. Gamble cut the power on the whole business and announced to the shocked crowd that the party was officially over.

He held up his hands to quell the cries of protest. "School rules. Twelve o'clock curfew."

There was much grumbling and, luckily, the vice-principal did not hear Mr. Morrison sending him to the dungeon. Reluctantly, the students began to file out of the gymnasium building.

Leaving the hot gym, they found a comfortable night with a welcome cool breeze. The sky was clear, and the towering lights of Manhattan surrounded them on all sides, looking somehow more imposing than usual. But most wonderful of all was the sight that met each student's eyes as he or she stepped out the door. The streets were filled with garbage trucks, heading busily in all directions, back at work and on their way to rid the city of its mountains of refuse. The garbage strike was over.

A good-natured cheer broke from the mass of students and, having no immediate plans, all twenty-six hundred settled themselves in and around the front of the school, all sitting quite comfortably on the hard pavement. They sat in quiet contentment watching the miracle unfold before them.

Suddenly, Daphne Sylvester's voice rose above the night. "Hey, where's Mike?" Several other voices took up the cry, and the students began to look around them.

Phil Gonzalez darted over to the parking lot, and when he returned, his face was a study in sadness. "He's gone! His car isn't there anymore! Mike's gone!"

"Gone?" Mr. Morrison snapped out of a light doze. "Mike's gone? But wait a minute! He can't do this! I still need him! Oh, no!" Before anyone could stop him, he galloped off into the night, howling, "Mike! Mike!" heedless of the hour and his kingly dignity.

Wayne-o was about to run after him but froze as a mournful sound wafted up in the school's courtyard. At the top of the front stairs stood Slim Kroy, blowing an emotional rendering of Taps into his tuba. All eyes were fixed on him, and when he took his mouth from the instrument, absolute silence fell. Not a single sound could be heard except the inspirational roar of the city's garbage trucks on their appointed rounds.

The entire population of Don't Care High, a force more than twenty-six hundred strong, sat in wordless contemplation of the loss of its president. There were some sighs, some tears, and perhaps a few muffled sobs, but no one spoke. It was a time of bittersweet perfection. It lasted five minutes, then ten, and fifteen. The tension was almost tangible, but no one would be the one to violate this silence — Mike's silence.

Then suddenly the brass-plated tuba was out of Slim's arms and bouncing noisily down the cement stairs, not missing a step. It seemed to cry out against the silence, saying *clang, bang, p-toom, boing, rattle, bam, fettuh-fettuh, futtuh-futtuh, clunk.* This last part came when the instrument hit bottom, coming to rest on its massive horn.

The tension disintegrated, and the students dissolved into mirth. Waves of laughter rose up among the lofty towers of the New York skyline.

15

At that point, the mass of students broke up, and precisely what transpired after that is unclear. It is unlikely that the Calvin Klein people ever figured out who spray-painted MIKE IS GONE, BUT HIS SPIRIT LIVES ON over their Times Square billboard. It is known, however, that a group of some forty Don't Care students was apprehended trying to storm Flash Flood's studio at Stereo 99 to tell Mike's story to the world. An even larger group of an estimated one hundred-plus was found trying to build a commemorative bonfire in Washington Square Park. They were stopped, however, before they could break more than four municipal bylaws. And many groups, too numerous to mention, were detained as possible street gangs, and ultimately taken home.

The night would go down in Don't Care history as the night Slim Kroy officially retired his tuba by borrowing earth from a park flower bed and planting geraniums in it — also borrowed. It was the night Daphne Sylvester received her first and last jilting, and the night in which Wayne-o ran up the largest single outfit dry-cleaning bill in his family's recollection. (It would later become his most successful photography project, a not-for-the-squeamish composition entitled "Wayne-o's Suit.")

It was the night Peter Eversleigh gave up stick for the second — and not at all final — time, a resolution that would last a scant seventy-two hours. Also that night, Phil Gonzalez broke his own record, putting a scratch on his father's Coupe de Ville measured at eleven feet, ten and three-eighths inches. Perhaps most significantly, it was the night Feldstein retired from the locker business in a touching ceremony in which his chair was dismantled, placed in a large box which had once held take-out Japanese food, and set adrift on the Hudson on an old raft someone had found by the shore.

Finally, it was the night Arthur Morrison slept under the stars on the roof of 106 Gordon Street, where he had gone to seek the man who could kindle school spirit in the hearts of his students.

Paul woke up around noon, aware of a headache, a stiffness in his legs, and a great queasiness in his stomach that could only have been caused by the tomato sauce patented under the name *Rocco* acting in combination with a massive licorice overdose. Last night had been a long one. With effort, he sat up in bed, cradling his chin in his hands, and reoriented himself.

Mike was gone. Regardless of the ridiculous aspects of Mike's rise to stardom, he really had touched all their lives. For Paul, Mike had dominated the majority of his thoughts in the span of his life in New York. What would it be like now without him? Paul tried to think back, but practically everything that was pre-Mike had taken place in Saskatoon. New York and Mike Otis had become inseparable in his mind. He sighed. It was hard to believe that, when school reconvened on Monday, Mike would not be there, and there was no way to find him.

He climbed out of bed and struggled to the window. Well, here was a kick. The building across the street was totally calm. It was the first time, day or night, that Paul had not been able to see one single weird thing going on over there. Even the Fifty-Thousand-Watt Family's apartment, normally illuminated twenty-four hours a day, was now dark. It proved that New York, too, could have a slow day now and then.

Leaving his room, he decided to postpone a much-needed shower in favor of drinking a few quarts of milk to sooth his digestive system. He was on glass number two when he saw the note on the kitchen table.

Dear Paul,

A terrible thing has happened. Auntie Nancy's dishwasher was installed improperly, and for some reason the water went up the wall and the ceiling caved in. Nancy needs me, and I will probably be with her all day as she is very nervous. Dad's working, so you're on your own. Have fun.

Love,
Mom

Paul wasn't surprised. It was almost nice to know that some things never changed.

He ate a breakfast which consisted of cold cereal and what was left of the milk, took a quick shower, dressed, and ventured out of the apartment. He and Sheldon had agreed to meet at one.

It was quite a brisk day, which appealed to Paul, especially since he didn't have to go through his mother's famous "You don't go out so soon after a shower" lecture. Just leaving the building was an enjoyable experience, as he no longer had to conduct himself through the maze of uncollected garbage that had been there only the day before.

The streets were filled with people, and in the crowd Paul felt he could lose himself. His thoughts returned to Mike. How long ago it seemed that Sheldon first picked the president at random in the infamous 200C hall of Don't Care High.

Paul reached the meeting place before Sheldon, so he seated himself on a bench to await his friend.

A young man walked by, carrying a large portable stereo, blasting out the best-known voice on the FM band.

"You're listening to Flash Flood, kicking off this holiday weekend with a blast! The holiday is that the garbage strike is over, which means that we can all look out our windows, even below the seventh floor! Traffic in from the suburbs today is backed up halfway to Alaska, but sit tight, you frustrated motorists, because the sun is shining through the smog and all systems are go in the greatest city in the world!"

The song that followed was one that Daphne had danced to at the party last night. Paul could see her still, the ultimate leading lady. He had tried so hard to be Steve, but when the dust cleared, there he was, still Paul. Yet Paul wasn't such a bad thing to be, under the circumstances. After all, he'd had a fifty percent share in bringing Mike to power. Well, at least forty percent. He sighed. With Mike gone, what was Paul now?

"Hey, Ambition." Sheldon jogged up to the bench. He took in the dejection on his friend's face and understood immediately. For a brief instant, the two could read each other perfectly. Then Sheldon perked up. "Don't look so grumpy. 'Mike is Gone, but his Spirit Lives On.' You know the slogan — you helped make it up. Funny thing about this world, it's chock-full of grand opportunities and all sorts of neat stuff. I can't think of a better place for the offspring of a genius and a guy with ambition." He gave Paul his most engaging smile. "But right now I could go for some food. I know a Chinese restaurant where the ribs are so delicious and so sticky — "

" — that they cement your jaw together," supplied Paul sourly.

"Yes! And do you know what else?"

"What?"

"It's not too far from this very spot. So if you'll just be so good as to follow me. . . ."

The two each polished off an order of ribs at Steinberg's Oriental Cuisine, then began walking downtown in companionable silence. On the street, an ancient Checker Cab, traveling seventy miles an hour, shot between two trucks with no space to spare, ran a red light where it was narrowly missed by a cement mixer, and screeched to a halt three-quarters of an inch behind a parked bus to pick up a fare. Paul, the boy from Saskatoon, would have gone home to spend the rest of the day in bed with a hot water bottle, but Paul the New Yorker simply joined in the applause from nearby pedestrians. The cab driver blinked his lights graciously and waved.

"Sometimes ordinary things can be glorious," Sheldon commented.

Paul was amazed at how heartily he agreed. He took a deep breath and found to his astonishment that the Steinberg's spareribs had gone down rather well. Where were the headache, dizziness, queasiness, cramps, gas pains, and heartburn he had come to know so well every time Sheldon recommended a restaurant? Could it be that he was developing a New York stomach? Given time and a little practice, he might even learn to digest the tomato sauce patented under the name *Rocco*.

With both ambition *and* a New York stomach, he would really be in good shape!

He was about to voice these thoughts to Sheldon when he caught sight of a dapper middle-aged man in front of a street-side vegetable stand. Paul stopped short and peered at the man's face intently. He was hard to recognize dressed in ordinary clothes, but yes, there was no doubt that this was the same man Paul used to watch from his bedroom window — the one and only Rabbit Man. Paul watched as his neighbor hand-selected and weighed out twenty pounds of carrots. A strangled laugh escaped Paul's lips. Saskatoon was a nice place, but only in New York could you run into Rabbit Man right on the street.

"Hey, Ambition," called Sheldon. "Are you all right?"

Paul smiled so wide it hurt his face. "Just fine," he replied exuberantly. "All systems are go in the greatest city in the world."

GORDON KORMAN

wrote his first book, *This Can't Be Happening at Macdonald Hall!*, when he was twelve years old. He has now written ten books for children, the most recent of which is *No Coins, Please*.

Don't Care High is the author's first book for young adults. It is based partly on his own experience in high school, where, he says, "the only way to get through alive was by laughing."

Gordon Korman was recently graduated from New York University's Dramatic Writing Program. A native of Ontario, Canada, he now lives in New York City.